"Don't treat me like a child, Adam," Diana said firmly as he lifted her in his arms.

All too aware of the ripe, feminine body he held, he gazed into her angry violet eyes. "Don't tempt me not to treat you like a child, Diana."

Confusion replaced her anger, and Adam felt a sense of pride at having, for the moment, saved his honor . . . and hers.

"Where's the bedroom?" he asked as he climbed the stairs.

"Second door on the right." She began to fidget. "Adam, I am capable of walking, you know."

He grinned. "Diana, let me enjoy this one rescue, at least."

She stopped squirming. "This is a rescue?"

"Well, it beats hell out of slaying dragons."

She opened her mouth to protest, but before she could say a word, her knight had pulled her close and laid siege to the sweet fortress of his lady's mouth . . .

WHAT ARE *LOVESWEPT* ROMANCES?

They are stories of true romance and touching emotion. We believe those two very important ingredients are constants in our highly sensual and very believable stories in the *LOVESWEPT* line. Our goal is to give you, the reader, stories of consistently high quality that may sometimes make you laugh, sometimes make you cry, but are always fresh and creative and contain many delightful surprises within their pages.

Most romance fans read an enormous number of books. Those they truly love, they keep. Others may be traded with friends and soon forgotten. We hope that each *LOVESWEPT* romance will be a treasure—a "keeper." We will always try to publish

*LOVE STORIES YOU'LL NEVER FORGET
BY AUTHORS YOU'LL ALWAYS REMEMBER*

The Editors

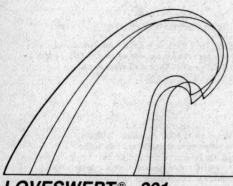

LOVESWEPT® · 201
Linda Cajio
Rescuing Diana

BANTAM BOOKS
TORONTO · NEW YORK · LONDON · SYDNEY · AUCKLAND

RESCUING DIANA

A Bantam Book / July 1987

*If you would be interested in receiving protective vinyl
covers for your Loveswept books, please write to this address
for information:*

Loveswept
Bantam Books
P.O. Box 985
Hicksville, NY 11802

ISBN 0-553-21821-2

Published simultaneously in the United States and Canada

PRINTED IN THE UNITED STATES OF AMERICA

O   0 9 8 7 6 5 4 3 2 1

I want to thank Rainy Anderson for being a spring, Anne Beltz for always listening, Carmele Olivo for all her patience and advice, Bev Haaf for her attention to small details, and Connie Flannery, who knows the reason why. Without their help, this book would not have been possible. I would also like to thank Adele Leone for being a terrific agent, and my editor, Elizabeth Barrett, for making the books better.

This book is dedicated to my father, Charles Camelier, the real storyteller in the family. He let me go through life thinking Lucy Goosey was a wanton. Thanks, Dad. I love you anyway.

One

"What's your latest game?"

"Will you go to the highest bidder?"

Backed up against the buffet table, Diana Windsor forced herself to tune out the almost rude questions the reporters surrounding her were asking. At the moment she owed herself a small celebration. Smiling privately, she toasted the end of her long search with a sip of champagne. The expensive wine had an odd sharpness she knew she'd never acquire a taste for, and the bubbles tickled her nose, making her want to sneeze.

It was worth drinking the stuff, though, Diana thought as she absently adjusted her wire-rimmed glasses on her nose. She'd just found the perfect face. Now all she had to do was persuade its owner to loan it to her.

"Is your appearance here an indication that Princess Di is on the market for the software companies?" a persistent reporter asked.

Diana wrinkled her nose at the nickname. A

few years ago someone in the press had christened her with it, as she not only had the same first name as the Princess of Wales, but also the royal British family was the House of Windsor. She was well aware that the nickname was a nasty inside joke too. The last person she resembled was the elegantly cool blonde princess. Glancing down at her navy skirt and white blouse, she decided she probably looked just like the out-of-touch hermit everyone in the computer industry thought she was. Should she have bought a new blouse or something for this reception? she wondered as she gazed around the luxurious, three-storied, glass-enclosed room. Everyone was more dressed up than she. It had been a long time since she'd attended a social event in the computer industry. Years ago the correct dress had been T-shirts and jeans, and this morning she had feared she would be overdressed in a skirt and blouse. . . .

The Face! Diana realized she was forgetting about the man whose face she needed. Rising on tiptoe, she tried to catch a second glimpse of the man, but it was impossible to see over the heads of the reporters, who kept her crowded against the buffet table.

"Darn it!" she muttered under her breath, wishing the pesky journalists would go bother someone else. She just had to have that face to study so she could get it exactly right. The Face was her Sir Morbid.

It really was odd, she thought, that the Face didn't resemble the type she'd originally been searching for. But the moment she had seen it, something inside her had known this was it. From her first glimpse of the man standing in a quiet spot by a window, she'd been inexplicably drawn to his craggy, virile features and his crooked smile.

She wondered what kind of man was behind that smile. . . .

"Excuse me," she murmured, setting her glass down on the buffet table. She began to gently squeeze her way between a man and a woman who were firing questions at her.

They jostled her back.

As she was pushed into the table, Diana realized two things at the same moment. One was that the reporters wouldn't allow her to escape without answering their questions. And two was that she was practically sitting on a large platter of shrimp pâté. She knew it had to be the shrimp, since she'd been standing next to the gooey stuff when the reporters had surrounded her. Now she could feel the wet mass beginning to seep through her skirt.

She tried to shove herself away from the table, but the reporters, almost shouting their questions now, had drawn even closer. One more time she attempted to move, but failed again.

Firmly settling onto the shrimp dish, Diana sighed. Something told her she was better off sitting unobtrusively in the hors d'oeuvres and answering a few questions. She certainly wasn't getting any closer to the Face and its owner by fighting the reporters.

"I'm here," she finally said to them, "because this is a reception to introduce the Omega computer to the public. Its chief designer, Bill Osmond, is an old friend of mine, and the computer's extraordinary breakthrough graphics and multitasking capabilities are a giant step forward in the industry—"

"Are you designing software for the Omega?" one reporter interrupted, and shoved a microphone in her face.

She blinked at the microphone, then began a cautious reply. "Probably—"

The reaction was instant and complete. Shouting to one another, the reporters turned with cattlelike grace and stampeded across the enormous reception room toward a small group of men, one of whom was Bill Osmond.

Diana blinked again, having no idea what she had said to make them so excited. She couldn't remember having said *anything*, and certainly nothing important. She'd only intended to say that the software companies who bought her programs would probably port them over to the Omega. Oh, well, at least she wouldn't be bothered by them anymore. Maybe shrimp pâté was an as yet undocumented lucky charm. And now that the reporters had left she could concentrate on the Face and the completion of her latest adventure game.

She grinned, pleased she'd finally be finishing months of concentrated and painstaking work. With each game she had created, she had challenged herself and, she hoped, the future players, by using new and different devices. But this time she'd done something no one had ever done before. She'd added voices that replied to the players' questions, and even gave hints when necessary. But she'd never been able to "draw" human features very well on the computer, so she'd hit upon the idea of using real faces for the program graphics. The face for Sir Morbid, her hero, had eluded her, though . . . until now.

Suddenly she remembered she still hadn't made contact with the man whose face she wanted to use. Groaning at her worse-than-usual absentmindedness, she began to look around the crowds of people, trying to spot him again.

"Excuse me," said a deep, gravelly voice.

Startled, Diana glanced up, then gaped in astonishment as she stared into the Face's deep brown eyes.

The man stared back at her, his straight, nearly black brows drawn together in a frown. As she'd first noticed, he was not truly handsome, but was extremely virile. His face was lean, rugged. Up close, she could see he was in his thirties. There was a cleft in his chin and his nose had a little bump that marred its straightness, indicating it had once been broken. The smile lines at the corners of his eyes and bracketing his mouth stood out sharply against his tan. His brown hair, brushed back from his forehead, had red and gold highlights.

As Diana gazed at the Face, a potent sensation sizzled along her nerve endings, accompanied by an awareness she'd never before felt. She found her attention focusing on the man's faintly musky scent, his tall, hard body under the three-piece beige suit, his fingers gently clasping the wine-glass. . . .

"Do you know you're sitting in the shrimp pâté?" he asked, jarring her from her mesmerized perusal.

"It keeps the reporters away," she said, not moving. Now that she'd been reminded of what she was sitting on, she noticed the damp chill spreading ever farther across her derriere. At the same time she felt a hot blush creeping up her neck. Of all the times to be caught in the shrimp! This really was beyond embarrassment, she thought. She decided the best way to save herself from her ridiculous situation was just to bluster her way through it. Besides, if she left to clean off her skirt, she might lose the man in the interim.

Politely she asked, "Why? Did you want some pâté?"

His face went blank for a moment; then he replied, "Maybe later."

"Good." She took a deep breath for courage and leaned closer to him. "Could I ask a favor of you? What I want isn't difficult, but it will be tiring."

"You want me to rescue you from the shrimp and carry you off into the ladies room, right?"

She chuckled. He even thought like a knight. "Forget the shrimp. What I need is you. It's very important to me, and I promise to give you credit when it's done. You're perfect, absolutely perfect. I've been searching for you all over, and I was getting desperate, but now I've found you. I'll pay, too. After all, it will take up several hours of your time. Just please say yes, because I don't know what I'll do if you say no."

It was his turn to gape in astonishment at her.

"Please," she repeated, smiling, hoping her rambling speech hadn't repelled him. "I've just got to have your face."

His face!

Adam Roberts shook his head in bewilderment. Whatever he'd been expecting her to ask of him, it certainly wasn't to borrow his face. In fact, he'd had the distinct impression she'd been asking for something entirely different. And that request would have been even more improbable than this one, considering what his brother Dan had told him about Diana Windsor.

According to Dan, who owned a software company, Diana Windsor was a brilliant, much-sought-after, yet hermitlike computer-games designer whom the media had dubbed Princess Di. Computer-software companies competed almost viciously to have a Diana Windsor game, as she had a reputation for producing best sellers. Dan claimed her "Space Pirates" had sold in the millions and was still in the top twenty on software charts after five years. Diana Windsor, it seemed, was the crown jewel of programmers.

Dan had also said she was called the Virgin Queen.

As Adam gazed at her sweet heart-shaped face and huge, guileless violet eyes, he silently cursed whoever had given her that particular nickname. Still, he had to admit there was something virginal about her. He'd been watching her ever since Dan had pointed her out among the reception guests. In her plain skirt and blouse, she stood out like a peahen among the expensively and lavishly dressed peacocks here. And she wasn't beautiful. Other than her eyes, there was nothing striking or exotic about her features, although he readily admitted he did like the way her nose turned up at the end. He also liked the dimple that had appeared when she smiled.

She had an aura of innocence, in spite of the most spectacular female body he'd ever seen. Her breasts were high and full, the rounded slopes beckoning to a man. Her waist was tiny, her stomach flat. Her hips flared dramatically, and her legs were shapely, her ankles trim. She had had her back to him at one point earlier, and he would have given a fortune to see her sable-brown hair let loose from its bun to tumble down the perfect line of her spine. More worldly females seemed to pale in comparison to her virginal allure, and he'd been drawn to her for that reason.

There was something very intriguing, too, about a woman blithely sitting in shrimp pâté while telling a man she wanted his face.

Naturally it was intriguing, he thought. It made one wonder whether she really was Diana Windsor or a psychiatric-ward escapee.

"Well, yes or no?" she asked.

No, Adam told himself. He was better off staying away from women who sat in shrimp and asked men for their faces. The whole business was crazy, and, besides, he still had no idea what she wanted with his face. But still . . . .

"Yes," he said, acknowledging that intrigue did win over common sense sometimes.

"Wonderful!" she exclaimed, smiling at him. "This is great! I finally have my Sir Morbid."

"Sir Morbid?"

"That's you."

Before Adam could question her further, she rose from her squishy seat. He watched in amusement as half the shrimp pâté rose with her.

"Yuck," she said, trying to see over her shoulder to access the damage. "I think I was better off staying put."

"Probably," he agreed, and reached for the serving knife next to the platter. "Shall I scrape?"

Diana hesitated for a moment, not sure what would be the least dumb thing to do right now. Then she realized the man was perfectly at ease with his suggestion. Sighing inwardly, she attempted to match his aplomb by giving him a lopsided grin. "Scrape away," she said. "Please."

He spread one hand across the back of her waist to keep her skirt steady, and Diana instantly felt the temperature in the room rise at least twenty degrees. She forced herself to stand as still as possible and ignore his almost intimate touch.

As he leaned forward and began removing the muck off her skirt, Adam realized she hadn't allowed him to do the dirty work as a kind of male/female game playing. There had been too much amusement in her eyes when she'd said "please." Sexually aware and interested women usually signaled something else, and Diana hadn't.

Lord, he thought, what if she really and truly were a virgin?

"Well, Diana, you've done it again."

Adam instantly stop scraping at the sound of a stranger's voice. Straightening, he saw a man smiling smugly at Diana, who let out a loud groan.

"Jim Griegson! You *would* have to show up now," she said in a disgusted tone, shaking her head.

"Problem?" Adam asked, coldly eyeing the man. Inwardly he was surprised at the sudden urge to protect his shrimp-sitting possible virgin.

"No problem," Griegson replied, raising his eyebrows. He pointed to the hors d'oeuvres now littering the floor. "What is that stuff, anyway?"

"Shrimp pâté," Diana said. "I suppose I'll be reading about this in 'The Last Byte.' "

Griegson laughed. "Definitely. Actually, Diana, rumor has it that you're writing programs exclusively for the Omega."

"I am?"

"That's what the reporters who talked to you are saying. Bill Osmond was very excited to hear it too. Seems even he didn't know anything about it."

"But I never said anything like that to them!" Diana wailed, throwing her hands up in exasperation. "They just shouted questions at me, pushed me into the shrimp pâté, then took off."

"So that's how it happened," Adam murmured as he watched consternation pull her forehead into a frown. He turned to the other man. "Obviously they didn't give her a chance to fully explain when they crowded around her earlier."

"So I realize. Who are you?"

Adam almost laughed at Diana's look of anticipation. He wondered if she was just realizing she'd never asked "Sir Morbid" his real name. "Adam Roberts."

Diana smiled.

"Adam Roberts . . ." Griegson said musingly. "Are you the new production manager with Peach Computers?"

"Not me. I barely know where a computer's 'on' switch is." He returned Diana's smile. "I'm an architect, and just a guest of a guest today. Who are you?"

Griegson raised his brows as if insulted by the question. "I'm Jim Griegson, and I write the 'Last Byte' column for *CompuWorld* magazine."

Adam's smile widened as Griegson then gave him a dismissive nod and turned back to Diana. "Well, you'd better remember whatever it was you didn't say, Diana, because they'll be back."

She rolled her eyes. "Wonderful. I'll just have to tell them it was all a mistake."

Griegson wagged a finger at her. "They'll never believe you didn't accidentally spill the beans. After nine years in this business you really ought to know how to handle the press. You old college hackers fall apart once the companies let you loose on the world."

"That's very funny coming from an old hacker like you, Jim. So what do I say to them?"

He grinned. "You don't have to tell them anything . . . if you give me the exclusive that you *will* be doing software for the Omega."

"But I—"

"You'll tell him nothing," Adam broke in, deciding she'd been badgered enough by Griegson. This was probably how she'd gotten into trouble with the other reporters. In her naïveté she would no doubt say something she didn't mean to—again. "What you will do, Ms. Windsor, is get the hell out of here. Then you don't have to say anything at all to anybody."

"But—"

"No buts." He took off his suit jacket and draped it around her shoulders. It fell to the middle of her thighs. "There. No one will notice you've given new meaning to the term *doggie bag.* Let's go."

Taking her elbow, Adam began to lead her away from the table. Griegson blocked them.

"Here we go again," Diana muttered to Adam.

"Diana," Griegson began in a soothing voice,

"wait a minute. I really do want to help you. I can calm down the others and make sure they don't start any false rumors. My column may contain occasional 'rumors,' but you know they're only facts leaked by the companies themselves. All I'm asking in return for the favor is that you answer a few of my questions. It will be good publicity for you."

Not giving Diana a chance to reply, Adam said, "I'll bet many a sucker has heard that before. But it is up to Ms. Windsor to decide who she will—or won't—talk to."

"Who the hell are you? Her bodyguard?" Griegson asked indignantly.

"It certainly looks that way," Diana said without rancor.

"And, as your new bodyguard, I suggest we get moving," Adam said, noticing several reporters closing in on them from the left. "The rest of the press is heading back this way."

"Bandits at two o'clock," Diana said, pointing out two more on their right.

"Surrounded by the Indians!" Griegson said gleefully, and began laughing.

One glance at Diana's worried face, and Adam knew she'd be scalped by those "Indians." He wondered what Sir Morbid would do to rescue the princess from fire-breathing dragons, then realized there was only one answer to that question.

He pushed Diana away from him and "accidentally" bumped into Griegson. With a loud squawk Griegson tripped, and banged into the buffet table. The buffet table, in turn, shuddered backward several feet across the marble floor. Unfortunately several plates and glasses decided to stay where they were. As they crashed on the floor, drawing everyone's attention, Adam stepped over to Diana and took her arm again. Her mouth was open in an O of astonishment.

"Let's go!" he ordered, pulling her away from Griegson.

Coming out of her shock, she half-ran with him past the rest of the surprised reporters and behind the buffet table to the nearest exit. In the ensuing commotion, nobody tried to stop them.

"Thank you," Diana said breathlessly as the double steel doors banged shut behind them. "I think."

"Believe me, you're welcome," Adam said, staring down the long, cinder-brick-lined corridor.

"I'm not very good with reporters," she admitted. "And I have no idea where we are. I came in through the hotel lobby to the reception."

Adam nodded, having used the same entrance. In the distance he could hear voices and the clatter of dishes. "This way sounds like the kitchen," he said. "We ought to be able to get out through there."

"But I really should say good-bye to a few people."

He turned to her in shock. "After what I just went through to rescue you?"

Diana groaned at the idiotic words that had just emerged from her mouth. She'd only been thinking of several people with whom she hadn't yet spoken. Somehow she wasn't managing to look like a mature, normal woman with this man. Shrugging, she said, "I guess we did say our good-byes, didn't we?"

"Damn straight we did."

Adam knew he should have curbed the impatience in his voice, but an unreasonable anger was building up inside him. He'd made a complete fool of himself in there by bumping the reporter into the buffet table. He'd never done anything like that before. His brother would probably disown him for humiliation by association. When Dan had asked him to come along with him today, Adam had only thought it would be interesting to see how a reception for a computer was conducted. If only he'd known what kind of trouble he'd be getting into. . . .

Damn his curiosity! He never should have approached Diana in the first place. He just couldn't understand his attraction to her, or his urge to protect her. Maybe agreeing to be this Sir Morbid—whoever he was—had brought out an old-fashioned streak of chivalry in him. Modern men didn't go around rescuing women on first meetings. The whole thing was so damned bizarre.

Suddenly Diana started to chuckle. "What you did to poor Jim Griegson! I know at least a dozen company presidents in there who are probably wishing they'd been the one to push him into the table. Jim's announced quite a few projects and rumors in his column that they'd love to strangle him for. Not all company 'leaks' are from top management, and most of Jim's aren't."

"I take it he's not a popular guy," Adam said, beginning to feel a little less angry. After all, none of what had happened was Diana's fault.

"Jim's extremely popular," she corrected him. "Everyone reads his column first in *CompuWorld* every week. They just hate to see themselves in his hot seat. I know I do."

"After what just happened, you'll probably be

RESCUING DIANA • 15

feeling the flames in his next column," Adam said with a wry smile.

"Along with himself falling into the buffet table." She chuckled. "I doubt he'll even mention it."

"Good."

"Well, I guess we should get going," she prompted.

He nodded. As they continued down the corridor, he told himself Diana was just a naïve programmer who'd never gotten used to the publicity her work generated. She really had needed rescuing today, and he'd been stuck as rescuer. No big deal. After all, it was only one rescue.

In the kitchen they found their way blocked again.

"Sorry. Can't go through here," a burly waiter said as he stood in the center of the aisle. The chefs and assistants glanced in their direction, but returned to their work when they saw someone was dealing with the intruders.

"Give us a break, pal," Adam said in frustration. Not again, he thought.

"Sorry."

Adam ground his teeth together in aggravation. Then an idea popped into his head. He leaned forward and said in a low voice. "You'd really be doing Ms. Streep a favor by letting her out through the kitchen. The reporters out there saw through her disguise and now they're on to her. She has to get to a producers' meeting right away."

"Ms. Streep?" the waiter said with a gasp. "You mean Meryl Streep, the actress?" He peered intently at Diana.

Adam smothered a grin when she looked as

surprised as the waiter. Diana certainly didn't know how to give an Academy Award performance.

"She'll be staying here while they film her latest picture in San Francisco," Adam added, hoping the waiter would believe him. "I'm sure the hotel's management would appreciate your helping us out."

Evidently the mention of the management was the deciding factor for the waiter. With a final, somewhat puzzled glance at Diana, he stepped aside and said, "Just go straight through and turn right. The door will let you out in the back parking lot."

"Thank you," Diana murmured as they hurried past the man.

"You're welcome, Miss . . . Streep," the waiter called out.

Dragging Diana with him, Adam started running. He was positive he wouldn't be able to contain his laughter until they were out of hearing distance. Diana was already giggling.

When the second set of double steel doors they'd encountered that day clanged shut behind them, Adam halted their escape run. He collapsed back against the doors, laughing.

"Meryl Streep!" Diana said, leaning next to him against the doors. "You really ought to warn a person before you turn her into a movie star." Considering her less-than-spectacular performance since she'd met Adam, she hoped she hadn't scared him away. Aside from needing his face, she really liked him. Vowing to act her age with him from now on, she continued, "I was so shocked when you said 'Ms. Streep,' I thought I'd give it all away!"

"You almost did with that look on your face," he

said, chuckling. "Fortunately the thought of getting into trouble with higher-ups meant more to that guy than letting a couple go through the kitchen."

"You know, this was exactly like the adventure games I do. You had to figure out logically how to get us past one blockade, and then the next. It even had a touch of a maze when we went down the corridor, made a turn, and ran up against another obstacle in the form of a waiter. And you got us past that one too."

With a charming grin she added, "You're going to make one heck of a Sir Morbid."

Adam groaned to himself as her smile triggered very unknightly urgings inside him. Diana might think he'd make a great Sir Morbid, but he had the uneasy feeling that he was going to have one hell of a time with his sword.

Two

"Lousy knights in shining armor," Diana muttered, glaring at the offending article in her latest issue of *CompuWorld*. "The fairy tales never said those clowns probably charged the princesses for hazardous duty after rescuing them."

She set her jaw as she read part of Jim Greigson's "The Last Byte" column again. "One of the highlights of the Omega reception was our own Princess Di, Diana Windsor, seen in a cozy tête-à-tête with Starlight Software President Dan Roberts's brother, Adam. Later Adam whisked her away for more 'private discussions.' Bet great things start happening to Starlight. But, folks, will they be in the boardroom or the bedroom?"

Darn that Jim Griegson, Diana thought as she slammed the magazine down on her desk. She folded her arms across her chest, leaned back in her swivel chair, and stared at the white ceiling of her workroom. She knew Jim had done this just to be nasty.

And darn that Adam Roberts, too, she thought furiously. She hadn't recognized his name at the reception, but she had heard of Starlight Software. Starlight had made several offers to buy her and her programs during the past year. Angelica, her cousin, lawyer, intermediary, and agent, hadn't liked Starlight's high-powered tactics and had broken off negotiations with them. Brother Adam was obviously an attempt to circumvent Angelica and get directly to her, Diana decided.

Absently adjusting her glasses on her nose, she sighed almost regretfully. She'd liked Adam Roberts. Truly liked him. He'd been charming, yet commanding and quick-witted when the situation had needed it. She'd felt . . . warm and safe with him. And there had been something special about him that affected her senses as no other man had. All week his image had continually intruded on her thoughts, interfering with her concentration on her work, leaving her oddly restless at night and barely touching her meals. She'd actually been impatient to see the snake again!

"So much for an IQ of one hundred seventy," she muttered in disgust. "You've got to be the dumbest bunny walking this earth!"

In her zeal to get him to pose for Sir Morbid, she'd never seen how she might have been playing into his hands. She admitted that in spite of just turning twenty-eight, she still needed street smarts in some areas. It was simply that she never thought about people having ulterior motives when they did things. She always did something because she wanted to. In Adam's case, she'd never once considered she had put him in a position where he could ask a favor of her.

Well, he had a surprise coming when he did. Reporters had always intimidated her, because she'd never felt at ease around them. She wasn't even at ease with regular industry reporters, whom she knew fairly well. She'd never had the knack, as some did, for saying a lot while not saying anything at all. But saying no to a software company's management was easy. She'd been doing it for over five years, since she'd first struck out on her own. Now she had the freedom to create her games as *she* liked, then sell them on the open market to the highest bidder.

She and Adam had arranged, after escaping the hotel, for him to come to her house on Saturday. That was today, and Adam still had never asked exactly what she wanted him to do.

Of course he wouldn't, she thought. She could ask him to high-jump to the moon, and he'd probably do it just to keep the lines of communication open. It was too late to cancel their work session. Besides, she still needed Sir Morbid's face. Being forewarned, though, she could handle Adam. And his brother.

Frowning a little, Diana wondered why the brother hadn't approached her at the reception in the first place. He was the logical one to do it. Why had it been Adam? He couldn't have known she'd wanted his face for her Sir Morbid. Even she hadn't known that until the moment she'd seen him. If she'd learned anything from the old BASIC language, it was that an *if* statement had to be followed by a logical *then* statement. It made no sense for Adam, who wasn't even in the business, to approach her about Starlight Software, when his brother was the president of the company. It made no sense for Adam to have approached her at all. Adam Roberts was definitely an *if* without a *then*.

She shrugged, dismissing her confusing thoughts. It really didn't matter who did the approaching. What did matter was that Adam and his brother thought she was easy prey. Obviously her reputation as a hermit had them thinking that she was vulnerable to a sneak attack. Well, she could be just as sneaky.

Her Sir Morbid wasn't turning out to be quite as she had envisioned, she thought, smiling crookedly. Still, it would be interesting to discover exactly how he intended to extract a victory.

Very interesting.

After parking the car in the gravel area in front of Diana's garage, Adam climbed out of his Trans Am and slammed the door.

For a moment he stared at Diana's modern redwood-and-glass house nestled in the wooded hills above Berkeley, California. It was a stunningly beautiful piece of tri-level architecture, with deep, sloping roofs, picture windows, and a wraparound deck that blended with its natural setting. Smiling, he silently saluted the architect who had designed the house with such care and created such harmony.

His smile faded as he thought about the house's owner. His brother had said Diana was successful, and as an architect Adam knew she had to be very successful to own a house like this. Diana had continually surprised him at their first meeting, and it looked as if their second would be no different. Since Monday, images of her had been popping into his head at the oddest times. She'd been funny, offbeat, and intriguing.

He frowned, remembering how overly interested his brother had been in Diana. After Adam had told Dan he'd be seeing Diana on Saturday, Dan had called daily to check if the meeting was still on. Yesterday afternoon he had called four times. There had been a kind of worried excitement in his voice. He had even called that morning. "Just asking," he'd said.

Adam wondered why his younger brother was so obsessed about the meeting with Diana. Dan acted as if Diana were the divine head of the church, and not a naïve, shrimp-sitting possible virgin.

But if Dan was so interested in Diana because of her games, Adam told himself, then he'd have to get them without his older brother's help. Adam's own business with Diana was personal, and he planned to keep it that way.

With that thought he crossed the drive and walked up the three deck steps to the front door. He had to ring twice before Diana opened it.

"Hi. Come on in, and we'll get started," she said before he could say hello. She pushed her wire-rimmed glasses up her nose. "My workroom's in the back."

As he followed her into the two-storied foyer, Adam grinned at her enthusiasm and at the glimpse he'd had of the front of her T-shirt. The University of California logo barely hid her unencumbered breasts, and her nipples were small pebbles against the thin knit. Her rich brown hair was in a loose ponytail that was rapidly becoming looser as it drooped on the nape of her neck. He let his gaze drift farther down to the back of her tight jeans and her slender bare feet. She looked downright earthy, and far removed from the "behind the times" innocent of Monday.

He sobered when he realized he would be in close proximity to her for hours. Why did she have to be so damned shapely? The knights of the Round Table would have tossed chivalry out on its ear if all the ladies of the realm had been built like Diana. He sensed, though, that his first impression of her as a naïve virgin was a more accurate one. He only hoped his willpower held up.

Wanting to dampen his growing awareness of her, he said, "This is a beautiful house, Diana. Who . . ."

His voice trailed away when they reached the threshold of her workroom in the back lower level. Adam stopped dead. As he gazed in astonishment at the room's contents, he wondered if he were about to enter the twilight zone. Frankenstein's laboratory had never looked so wild. The workroom was enormous, running the width of the house, and contained the largest collection of computers he'd ever seen. There had to be at least twenty of the machines in all sizes sitting atop various desks and tables along two walls. Even a couple of commercial arcade games—big, boxlike things about six feet tall, with glowing screens to tempt players to part with their quarters—competed for space. The other two walls were lined with floor-to-ceiling bookshelves crammed with books. The electronic jungle was so overwhelming that the double sliding glass doors along the back actually looked squished.

As his first surprise wore off, Adam became aware that there was order amid the chaos. The books and magazines weren't just shoved any which way into the bookcases, but were neatly shelved. The manuals on the tables and desks were primly stacked or standing between bookends. Although wires seemed to snake everywhere, they were neatly bound together in an effort to keep them under control. In fact the room and its contents were scrupulously clean, and everything seemed to have a place.

"Don't worry," Diana said, chuckling. "Nothing bites."

"I hope not," Adam said, cautiously entering the room. "Do you actually use all of these?"

"I only use these for most of my preliminary work," she said as she crossed the room to where three computers sat bunched together on an oversized table. A single swivel chair with rollers sat in front of it. "The others are different models currently on the market or outdated older ones that I don't have the heart to get rid of."

"My brother would think this was computer heaven," Adam said, still trying to take it all in.

She turned around, her eyebrows raised above the top of her glasses. "Oh? Your brother likes computers?"

He laughed, remembering how Dan had always been hunched in front of a computer when he was a teenager. "He loves them. He has his own software company in Seattle. Maybe you've heard of it. It's called Starlight Software."

She shrugged. "I'm afraid I don't get out as much as I used to. What kind of stuff is he doing?"

"Educational and game programs," Adam replied, forcing himself to keep his mind on the conversation. He didn't remember Diana's mouth looking so provocative on Monday . . . or the intriguingly stubborn tilt to her chin . . . or the mysterious depths of her violet eyes. He cleared his throat. "I was Dan's guest at the reception."

In the ensuing silence there was a funny look on her face. Adam frowned. It was almost as if she were expecting him to say something more, and he had no idea what he was supposed to say. He'd exhausted his knowledge of his younger brother's business. Since both of them were busy building their respective companies, they didn't get a chance to talk very often anymore. When they did, though, Dan usually talked about how business was, not what it was.

Unfortunately, too, Adam hadn't been exaggerating very much on Monday when he'd said he barely knew where a computer's "on" switch was. He did know that—but only on his firm's two computers. His partner had had to teach him how they worked. If the smallest thing went wrong, though he was instantly yelling for help. Without fail, the damn machines always beeped like crazy and acted as if he'd just taken an ax to them. There were times when he wished he had.

When Diana continued to look expectantly at him, he asked, "What am I supposed to do as this Sir Morbid?"

"Not very much," she said, giving him a wry smile. "I won't have you jousting with windmills, I promise. The computer just needs your face."

"The computer needs my face?" he repeated in confusion. It sounded as if he were about to be the computer's next meal.

"Right." She pulled a chair in front of the sliding doors. "I have a certain face in mind for each of the characters in my newest game, but I'm lousy at drawing faces freehand on the computer. They all wind up looking like Richard Nixon."

Adam chuckled.

"So what I want to do is take some pictures that I can sort of enhance." Straightening, she tapped her finger against her chin for a moment. "Now, where did I put that armor?"

"Armor!" he exclaimed, wondering what he'd gotten himself into.

"You're a knight of the Oblong Table, so you've got to wear some armor, and I can't draw that any better than I can draw faces. Aha!"

As she walked across the workroom to get Adam's costume, Diana breathed an inward sigh of relief. She was grateful to put a little distance between them. Ever since he'd walked in the front door, her body had acquired that odd tenseness she'd first felt on Monday, and her stomach had flip-flopped every time she'd looked at him. More and more she was aware of Adam as a man . . . and of herself as a woman. She decided she'd hidden her reaction to him fairly well. He hadn't seemed to notice anything wrong with her. But she'd never get through the afternoon if she couldn't control her emotions. Darn it, she thought. Surely what she knew about him would have killed any attraction to him.

Concentrate on the task at hand, she told herself as she reached a desk on the far side of the workroom. If her disturbing thoughts continued she'd probably do something idiotic, and that would only confirm the unflattering image she was certain Adam had of her. She knelt down and pulled a large costume box from under the desk. On top of the desk was Charlie, the computer that controlled her house's elaborate burglar-alarm system. It had seemed appropriate for her modern armor to guard its more ancient version.

Flipping the lid off the box, she motioned Adam over. "It's just the helmet and breastplate. I got it from a costume shop in Berkeley. I hope it fits. It's only a medium."

Squatting down on his heels next to her, he touched the glistening metal. "Good Lord, Diana! This is real!"

"Well, it is steel," she said, suppressing her laughter. "But it's as thin as paper and very lightweight. You'll look wonderful, Adam. Go ahead and put it on."

"Not until you tell me exactly what you're going to do," he said sternly.

"For goodness sake! You don't have to act as if I'm asking you to sack Camelot!" she said indignantly, glaring at him. "I'm only going to take some pictures of you in the armor."

"No sword fights with a fake dragon?"

"Not even a princess to kiss."

The change on his rugged features was instant. The suspicion was gone, and in its place was mischievous amusement.

Almost in awe Diana stared at him. It was as if she had unknowingly challenged him in some way, and he was now taking up the gauntlet she'd thrown down. Suddenly he didn't seem at all the safe, gentle protector of Monday. She sensed that behind the too-innocent grin and the mirthful brown eyes was a relentless hunter stalking his next victim on a very personal level. Part of her wanted to run like hell, but the other part wouldn't move—not even for an earthquake. Her brain couldn't cope with the conflicting signals it was receiving, so it shut down. Blank.

"Princesses pop up at the damnedest times, Diana," he murmured, lifting the armor out of the box. "I should know."

As his cryptic words broke the spell over her, Diana sank back on her heels in relief and regret that everything was normal again. She didn't know why she should regret losing those magical seconds, but she did. She firmly told herself to remember his brother and Starlight Software. If she kept gawking at him like a moony teenager, he'd think she was a pushover, for goodness sake! She gave herself a stern lecture to act like the mature woman she ought to be.

Adam rose and held out his free hand to help her up. When she put her hand in his strong grip, an arc of fire shot up her arm. She realized everything wasn't quite back to normal. Obviously lectures about not letting this man affect her wasn't quite as expedient as good, old-fashioned no touching.

"I guess we should get started," she said brusquely, managing to slip her hand from his without awkwardness. "I'll finish setting up by the doors while you get into the armor."

Quickly walking away, Diana felt his gaze on her back. A tingling sensation rippled through her, and her nipples began to harden. She found herself wishing she'd worn a bra, and redoubled her efforts to calm her surprisingly traitorous body. Good old-fashioned no touching, with a little distance thrown in besides, wasn't quite enough, she admitted. But it helped—at least he couldn't see her nervousness. She hoped.

She turned on the two work lamps she'd set up earlier for backdrop lighting, then placed her rented video-tape camera on its tripod and looked through the tiny viewer. Fumbling with the knobs, she adjusted the camera's height several times before she was satisfied with the arrangement. As she straightened, a sudden string of curses filled the room.

Surprised, she turned around to find Adam, bent like a contortionist, struggling to hold the front breastplate against his chest with one hand while barely hanging on to the back plate with his other.

"Let me help you," she said, laughing.

"How the hell did those guys get into these tin cans?" he asked, beginning to hobble toward her.

She grabbed the back breastplate just as he lost his grip on it. Buckling the shoulders together, she asked, "Why didn't you just slip it over your head?"

"Because it wouldn't fit!" he said in a choking voice, and tugged at the neckhole. "Loosen the buckles so I can breathe!"

Grinning, Diana readjusted the buckle on each shoulder to its last notch. She giggled at his huge sigh of relief and helped him with the side fastenings. She also resisted the urge to let her hands linger at the task.

"Okay," she said when the armor was securely on, "go sit on the stool and put on your helmet."

He gave her a skeptical look before placing the helmet over his head. The fit was better; the helmet completely covered his head and neck. He pushed up the slitted visor and said, "There damn well better be a princess after all this!"

She gave him a nudge in the direction of the stool. "Come on, it can't be that bad."

"Wanna trade places?"

"I don't have the Sir Morbid look. And besides," she added, following him to her makeshift studio, "I have to work the camera."

He sat down. "Why are you—"

His visor suddenly snapped shut. Diana burst into laughter, and he raised the visor and glared at her.

"Where did you get this thing? Guillotines Incorporated?"

"Just keep your nose tucked in and you'll be okay," she said, wishing she'd had the film rolling. With a last giggle she put her eye to the viewer, then fiddled with the lens until she had the focus exactly right. Pressing a button, she started the camera, then straightened and casually crossed her arms over her chest.

Adam glanced at the camera. "Before I was so rudely interrupted by my visor," he said, "I was going to ask why you're using a video camera and not a regular one."

"I can transfer a video tape into the computer and freeze-frame what I want," she explained. "Then I can just paint over the picture and use it as part of the graphics of my game. I can't do that with a photograph."

"So all I have to do is sit here and—"

The visor snapped shut again. Diana doubled over with laughter. She hoped he'd been looking directly at the camera when it had happened. The film would be priceless if he had. Sir Morbid couldn't have done better, she thought.

"—and keep my mouth shut," Adam finished as he lifted the visor.

He grinned at her, and her stomach did flip-flops again. In that moment Diana realized that in spite of what she knew about him, she liked him just as much now as she had at their first meeting. More. She was still distressed by the potent attraction that continued to draw her to him. Worse, that attraction was growing stronger with each minute she spent in his company.

Adam Roberts, she decided, was becoming as complicated as one of her adventure games. She wasn't sure she liked that.

She wasn't sure at all.

Three

"All this knighthood has made me hungry," Adam said as he pulled off his helmet and wiped the film of sweat from his forehead. "I know the perfect place we can go to for an early dinner. The Tapestry Room."

Diana hesitated before answering. In spite of the underlying currents constantly pulling inside her, she had managed to be a mature professional during Adam's filming. She wondered, though, if she should press her luck any further. Surely she had shown him his job of getting her to come to work for Starlight wouldn't be as easy as her reputation implied.

But Adam had made no move to coerce her into working for his brother. Not a word. She had given him plenty of opportunities, too. She silently admitted she was becoming very curious about what enticement he would use. Would it be a Ferrari or a BMW? A condo in Hawaii or one in Mexico? A large chunk of stock or a cut of the profits? Some software companies offered the most amazing things to recruit a programmer or designer. Maybe Adam would come up with something unique and completely new. Whatever he had in mind, this had to be the real purpose of his seemingly casual dinner invitation. It might be interesting to see how much more his methods of persuasion would differ from other companies'. They'd certainly been different so far.

"I've never been to the Tapestry Room," she said, ignoring the little voice in her head that mumbled something about curious cats.

"It's very medieval, so as Sir Morbid's creator you'll feel right at home," Adam said. His gaze lowered to her T-shirt. He stroked his jaw for a moment, then added, "I'm afraid you'll have to change, though. The Tapestry Room is casual, but not that casual."

"Oh." She glanced down at her T-shirt, jeans, and bare feet. "I guess I should."

"Wear something bulky. It can be cold in there," he said with a wry grin.

After Diana disappeared, Adam prayed she owned a sweater made by Omar the tentmaker. He'd never survive the rest of the evening if she wore *anything* that remotely hugged her body. The only things that had saved him from disgrace today were the hot lights and the hotter armor in which he'd been encased. They had constantly distracted him from Diana, and he was grateful for that. All afternoon he'd felt that innocent aura of hers. Most men would have backed away from it, but he acknowledged it was one of the things that drew him to Diana. He'd never met a woman quite like her before. She was a unique blend of naïveté and sexiness, and he found himself continually pulled to her. Yet he'd quickly realized he'd have to take things very slowly with her.

Attempting to turn his thoughts in another direction, he wandered over to the two coin-operated arcade games. The coin slots had been removed, and seeing that one of the games was her famous "Space Pirates," he pressed the start button. Suddenly a horde of tiny spaceships zoomed across the screen, firing their torpedoes in time to the fast-paced music.

Grinning like a kid, Adam slapped buttons and rammed the joy stick back and forth, trying to shoot the enemy into the great beyond before he was shot. He lost his ships in rapid and devastating succession. Obviously the game called for quick reflexes and quicker strategy, he thought as the screen flashed his miserable score points. It asked him if he wanted to play again.

With a silent "No, thanks," he turned his back on the machine and walked over to the three computers atop a single table. Diana had said they were her actual working computers, and he wondered why she used three. After all, she was only one person. He caught sight of the stack of computer paper on the edge of the table and began flipping through the print-outs. They were filled with numbers and what looked like gibberish to him. He raised his brows, wondering how anybody could understand it. Yet he knew Diana could.

Amazing, he thought. She didn't look like a brain trust.

Hearing her steps in the hallway, he let the

papers fall back into place and turned around. When she entered the room, he smiled in pleasure. Her sable-brown hair had finally been let loose to caress her shoulders, and while her beige cable-knit sweater wasn't quite the size of a tent, it did downplay the tantalizing shape of her breasts. Her trousers were nice and, thank heavens, not tight-fitting, unlike her jeans. She looked attractive, but without the obvious sexual allure.

As he gazed at her, he realized there was a lot more to admire about Diana. She was refreshingly straightforward, obviously brilliant at her craft, and comfortable with who and what she was.

Diana Windsor, he decided, was one princess he planned to keep to himself.

"Ready?" he asked, walking over to her.

She nodded. "Sure you don't want to wear the armor?"

He grinned. "Believe me, the Tapestry Room doesn't need a Sir Morbid."

When they entered the Oakland restaurant a short time later, Adam glanced at Diana and smiled. Her eyes were round with wonder as she gazed at the Tapestry Room's gray stone walls and stained-glass windows. Wall hangings depicted medieval battles and hunting scenes. Shields, lances, broadswords, and other weapons hung from the walls. The flagstone floor was even strewn with rushes in an effort to duplicate a castle's great room.

"Two full suits of armor," Diana said almost reverently, pointing to the display standing guard in the restaurant's entryway.

"Wait until you see the bar," Adam said. "The bartenders are dressed in chain mail."

"In a minute. I just want to look more closely at this armor," she said, and walked over to one of the statues. She stroked the right gauntlet, which clutched a triangular banner of red silk.

Adam smiled at her, then turned to the hostess, who was dressed in a velvet gown and wimple.

"Table for two, please," he requested, then added, "Could you give us a few minutes, though?"

The hostess looked at Diana and smiled. "No problem, sir."

The hostess bustled away, and Adam glanced around with a new appreciation at the restaurant's familiar decor. He'd had more than one meal here since establishing his architecture firm in Oakland three years before. Grinning, he wondered if he'd unconsciously been in training for the role of Sir Morbid all that time.

"Adam!" Diana suddenly whispered from behind him.

He turned to discover her holding the armor's left gauntlet in her hand, a look of panic on her face.

"How did that happen?" he whispered back, striding over to her.

"I don't know!" she replied in a low tone as he took the gauntlet from her. "I just touched it and it came off."

Trying to fit the metal glove back onto the armored sleeve, he muttered, "You must have twisted it or something."

"But I didn't!" she whispered. "Here, let me hold this still for you."

She grasped the sleeve just above the wrist to

steady it. Adam's jaw dropped in astonishment as the whole sleeve instantly came free in her hands. She stared at the sleeve for a moment, then looked up at him.

"I'm sorry, Adam. I guess you can dress me up, but you can't take me anywhere," she said in a small voice.

Fighting laughter, he shook his head. "If all the ladies needed as much rescuing as you, Diana, knighthood never would have gone out of business. Gimme that thing!"

She shoved the sleeve into his hands. He bent down and very gently placed it and the gauntlet on the pedestal base, directly between the statue's armored feet.

Straightening, he looked at her. "I don't suppose you want to stay for dinner now, do you?" he asked dryly.

She looked around in embarrassment. "No, not really."

As they were walking across the parking lot toward his car, she sighed. "Honestly, Adam, I have no idea how that arm came off."

"I do," he said as they reached his car. He unlocked the passenger door and opened it. When she was seated in the gray velour seat, he added, "As I said before, it's a good thing princesses are naturally klutzy. Otherwise we Knights of the Oblong Table would be out of business."

He shut the door before she could answer. Striding around the car, he thought with amusement that he was giving not just his face, but his whole body to the role of Sir Morbid. He wondered if Diana had always been in such need of rescuing— and who had been rescuing her before him.

After he'd climbed into the driver's seat and started the Trans Am, she swiveled to face him.

"I am not a klutz," she said. "But I think you're a jinx."

"Me!" he exclaimed. "That armor came apart in *your* hands, not mine. And I wasn't the one sitting in shrimp mold making a spectacle out of myself. And I certainly wasn't the one who had to be rescued from the reporters."

She pushed her glasses back up her nose. "That was the first time anything like that happened to me, and it was also the day I met you. In fact, whenever something happens, I'm with you. Now, how do you explain that?"

"I don't," he muttered.

Out of the corner of his eye, he could see her stony expression. "Look, Diana," he said in a gentle voice, "let's just forget about the armor and everything else, okay?" He tucked a strand of silken hair behind her ear. "After all, we were together this afternoon without experiencing a single unexplained phenomenon. No disasters with the camera, no getting stuck in the helmet, no exploding computers."

Diana swallowed as his fingers tenderly brushed against her cheek. It wasn't fair, she thought. Of all the men in the world to suddenly have this sizzling reaction to, it had to be Adam. Why him? He was the *wrong* man, plain and simple. Adam Roberts was dangerous. And it had nothing to do with his connection to Starlight Software. He was just dangerous as a man.

Somehow, too, she always managed to look like a female Barney Fife around him. Hardly the cool professional that she was. That armor coming off had been embarrassing enough, but then she had made things worse by accusing him of being a jinx because she had done something dumb. She groaned silently. In less than five minutes she had completely shredded the in-control-woman image of the afternoon. She should have said no to dinner, but she had really thought she could handle it. Dumb Diana, she berated herself. She'd been lulled into a false sense of security, and she should have known better.

"Peace, Diana?" he asked, his deep voice rumbling over the racy whine of the car's engine.

"Peace," she agreed. It was easy to say, she thought. She wouldn't be seeing him again after tonight. There was no reason to. Her curiosity was dead concerning his probable mission for his brother's company. And her curiosity about him in other ways was too aroused.

"Now let's find a *decent* restaurant," he said, smiling at her.

"Fine," she replied, telling herself that to refuse would only be ridiculous at this point. Mentally crossing her fingers, she vowed not to touch a thing.

It wasn't until after their dinner at another restaurant that Diana realized Adam had never brought up business at all. In the relaxed atmosphere, without a single piece of medieval memorabilia in sight, she'd again forgotten the real purpose of his pursuing her acquaintance. Instead, she had just enjoyed his company, enjoyed being with Adam the man. They'd even laughed and teased each other about the Tapestry Room incident.

Now, as he parked his car in her darkened drive, she wondered when he would get around to dropping the proverbial other shoe. Maybe he'd been trying to catch her off guard with all this friendly companionship. Maybe, by some miracle, he actually thought she wouldn't be quite as easy to persuade as her nerdy-hermit image indicated. No, she was reaching for a dream on that one, she admitted. Fortunately, her amnesia had only been temporary. Good thing she was in the programming business, because she would have made a lousy James Bond.

"Time for all good princesses to be back in their castles," Adam said as he helped her out of the car.

She smiled at him. "Thank you for dinner. The lasagna was delicious. And thank you, too, for playing Sir Morbid, Adam. I know I took up a good deal of your time, so let me pay you for it."

"You don't owe me anything. It was an experience I wouldn't have missed." He chuckled dryly.

"But I insist."

Without answering, he took her elbow and guided her across the drive and up the steps of the deck. Diana grinned at herself, thinking that Adam had all the instincts of a chivalrous knight. She hadn't had so many doors opened for her in her life. Still, she would pay him for his time. She didn't like the idea of owing anybody for anything. And in Adam's case, not owing him was imperative. She certainly couldn't leave herself open to any machinations he might try on Starlight's behalf. If the Starlight people wanted her games, they'd have to play fair and go through Angelica.

When they reached her front door, she started to fish in her purse for her keys. Adam laid his hand over hers, stilling it.

"There is one payment I want for services rendered," he said softly.

She lifted her head and stared at him as his voice sent warning tingles up her spine. She forced herself to stay cool and collected.

"Oh?" she asked, hating the telltale squeak in her voice.

"I only want one kiss from the princess."

Before she could put a safe distance between them, his mouth settled firmly on hers. In desperation she jerked her head back. He only smiled and, threading his fingers through her dark hair, pulled her to him again.

His lips were warm and gentle, creating similar feelings inside her. Diana slowly relaxed, and her eyelids fluttered closed of their own accord. His mouth fitted itself to hers and exerted more pressure, parting her lips. His tongue rubbed against hers, boldly persuading her to submit to his possession. Almost timidly, she stroked back. The sensations running through her veins suddenly intensified, becoming hot, fierce waves pounding against her skin. She clutched at his shoulders as if for an anchor, her fingers digging into them. His mouth slanted hungrily across hers, his arms becoming iron bands around her back as he pressed her against the length of his hard body.

She felt her whole being jolt in response, and, as she helplessly kissed him back, she knew she never wanted the spinning and swirling to stop. But they did.

She blinked in confusion when slowly, almost reluctantly, he lifted his lips from hers. He didn't let her out of his embrace, though. Instead he tucked her cheek against his chest and rested his chin on the crown of her head.

"Obviously the Brothers Grimm left out the good parts of their fairy tales," he said in an amused voice. "Or else they never passed the censorship committee."

"What censorship committee?" she asked, snuggling closer to the heat of his chest. She could hear his heart beating under her ear.

"The guys who cut the pow out of the princesses' kisses in the fairy tales."

"Oh." Diana didn't know what else to say. She was astonished that he'd evidently been as affected by the kiss as she had.

"This is getting too . . . comfortable," he said. "Get your keys out, princess, and unlock the drawbridge."

"Please don't call me that," she said while fumbling through her purse again for her keys.

"Seems to me you've been qualifying for the role lately."

Her face heated in embarrassment as she finally pulled her keys from the purse. They instantly slipped through her fingers to the deck. Diana calmly looked around for the nearest rabbit hole to climb into. Adam certainly seemed to bring out the klutz in her, she thought.

He bent and picked up the keys. Handing them back to her, he quipped, "Looks like I'm on a rescuing roll."

"I just didn't want you to lose your touch," she replied, refusing to allow her mortification to show.

He took her right hand, gently spread her fingers back, and dropped the cool metal keys into her open palm. Then he closed her fingers around them but didn't release her, and she looked up at him in puzzlement. Even in the dark shadows she could see the smile playing across his mouth.

"Some princesses never know when to stop," he said.

She resisted the urge to ask him what he meant, sensing she was better off not knowing. She pressed the shut-off sequence for her burglar-alarm system, then unlocked the front door.

Turning back to face him, she said, "Thank you for your help, Adam, and for a lovely evening. Good night."

He leaned forward and kissed her swiftly. "That was a bonus for overtime."

"Good night, Adam," she said firmly, and stepped inside.

Leaning back against the oak door, she breathed a sigh of relief. Adam Roberts was too contradictory and confusing, she decided. He'd hypnotized her, too. Somehow he'd managed to keep her relaxed and make her like him more and more. He'd soothed all her inner qualms about him with his no-pressure companionship. And he had practically drugged her with that kiss. He certainly was taking his time before he moved in for the kill.

Her contrary heart protested that she was condemning the man on only a rumor in Jim Griegson's column. She wondered for a moment if she could be wrong about him. He had never once attempted to make a deal for his brother or Starlight Software. In fact, he hadn't mentioned them at all that night.

Maybe he wasn't involved in his brother's company, she thought. Maybe their first meeting had been coincidental, and not deliberate, as she'd suspected. Maybe he was just a man with a chivalrous soul, willing to help out a woman in need. That, at least, made more sense than his participating in some elaborate plan to get her games for his brother's company.

She sighed again and rubbed her temples, willing away all thoughts of computer skullduggery. It didn't matter whether Jim's rumor was true or false anyway. Adam hadn't asked to see her again. Services had been rendered in full, and that was all she'd wanted from him in the first place.

She ignored the little voice inside her that said he had rendered them very well.

Four

Exhausted, Diana leaned back in her padded swivel chair to ease her cramped, aching muscles. She was dimly aware that her clothes—the sweater she'd worn to dinner with Adam and the jeans she'd changed into after she got home—felt a bit grubby. She pushed her glasses up on the top of her head and rubbed her bleary eyes, then surveyed the picture of Adam on her computer's monitor screen.

She smiled. Although it had taken hours to repaint his face carefully with the computer's electronic paint program, the results were exactly as she'd hoped. Adam's face was still Adam's face. Well, sort of. At least it didn't look like Richard Nixon.

She rubbed her eyes again, wondering what time it was. She realized she must have worked through the night, since sunlight was filtering through the heavy curtains on the glass doors. She knew from past experience, though, that it could be any time of day.

"I lose more weekends this way," she muttered good-naturedly.

Deciding to take a short break, she rose from the chair and stretched her arms over her head. As her body creaked and protested, she acknowledged she *had* been working much too long. But she had finally picked the different expressions she wanted for her game and had actually begun the painting-over process. The game was nearly done.

And in the hour's worth of continuous tape of Adam that she'd analyzed, she'd never once seen even a nuance of an expression that said he was anything more than a man playing knight for a day.

She groaned, remembering how many times she'd caught herself just staring at one of the pictures of his face, and how she'd had to force herself to think of him as work. But after what she'd seen—or rather hadn't seen—she was more confused than ever about Adam. Was he involved in some scheme to get her to sell to Starlight, or wasn't he? She'd been trained to think in a logical, sequential manner, and that training was useless for this. She just didn't know how to approach the problem. If she ever saw him again, maybe she should just ask him . . . but would she believe a denial?

She groaned again, wishing she'd had more experience with men—

"Intruder alert! Intruder alert!" a metallic voice intoned, shattering the quiet of the workroom.

Klaxons blared and a calliope of dogs began barking viciously.

"Omigod!" Diana gasped, startled and deafened in the same moment.

The noise was her computer's first alarm. She forced herself to calm down, drawing in a deep breath, but her heart still insisted on pounding wildly.

Probably an animal had tripped one of the sensors scattered on her property, she thought. Charlie, her household computer, would continue the klaxons and recorded barking dogs for five more minutes before shutting itself down. Its second alarm would be triggered if and when someone actually touched one of the doors or windows. Not only would the klaxons and dogs start again, but Charlie would also call the police. If it wasn't a raccoon or a deer . . .

"Just stay calm and stay in the house!" she told herself, while swallowing back her fear.

Suddenly someone began pounding furiously on her glass doors, and she screamed.

"Diana! It's me! Adam!"

"Oh, Lordy," she muttered, placing her palms against her heaving chest in relief.

She raced over to Charlie and, fingers flying over the keys, turned off the alarm system before it could dial the police. Then she ran to the doors, flung the curtains back, and unlocked the glass panels.

Sliding the doors open, she glared at her intruder and asked, "Why didn't you knock at the front door?"

"When did you get dogs?" Adam asked, glaring back as he stepped into the room.

"It's just a recording," she said, rubbing her

suddenly aching forehead. Only Adam, thank goodness, she thought.

"A recording! It sounded like the hounds of hell were after me!"

At his astonished expression, she began to giggle. "It's supposed to scare off burglars, among other things."

"It scared ten years off my life, woman!" he exclaimed.

"Which is what you deserve for leaving the front-door area," she retorted indignantly. She couldn't imagine why he was so annoyed, when *he* had been the one to set off the alarm.

His brown eyes narrowed, and he pointed a finger at her. "Which I would not have had to do if you had bothered to answer twenty minutes' worth of pounding on that same door."

Diana felt a hot flush scald her cheeks. She looked down at the floor and muttered, "I didn't hear you."

There was a silence, and she finally glanced up at him. His hands were on his hips and he was shaking his head.

"Just tell me one thing," he said. "How did I set off the alarm? All I did was walk around the house to see if you were home."

Becoming aware that this was *Adam* standing in front of her, Diana belatedly realized how awful she must look. She wished she could just press a button and magically change into Miss America. Since that was impossible, she decided the best thing to do was just act mature and ignore her appearance.

Edging away from him so she wouldn't offend more than necessary, she said, "Only the front drive and the door are cleared for visitors. There are light sensors everywhere else, and my computer automatically assumes anyone who triggers one is up to no good, so it sounds the first alarm. It can't distinguish between animals and people. The barking-dogs recording usually scares off the animals—"

"I've got news for you, honey," Adam interrupted, grinning. "People won't see the inside of their bathrooms for days after hearing that klaxon either."

"Adam!" she exclaimed. "Let's just say I went a little crazy when I built the system."

"A little! A jailbreak from Alcatraz couldn't have set off that much noise."

"Why are you here, Adam?" she asked, folding her arms across her chest.

He hesitated a moment before answering. "I have to go visit a site, and just thought I'd drop by first."

Silently Adam cursed the lame excuse. It sounded like something a teenage boy would say to a girl he had a crush on, in the hope of sounding suave and nonchalant. At thirty-four he had no business acting like a teenager.

"Actually, I came to see you," he admitted. "Though I really should go up to Richmond today. We've been asked to bid on an office complex near there. Hey, is that me?"

Having caught sight of the picture on the computer screen, he walked over to it, then stared in shock. Of course he'd seen pictures of himself before, but they always looked somewhat like the face he saw in the mirror every day. Painted over liberally, the human colors exaggerated, he now looked like an overconfident, boorish . . . hero. There was no other word that better described the haloed burnished-gold locks, the jaw so square that it looked ready to crack, or the gleam literally bouncing off the blinding smile.

"It's perfect," Diana murmured lovingly as she looked over his shoulder.

"Perfect!" He turned and stared at her. "I look like an idiot!"

"Not you, Adam," she corrected him. "Sir Morbid. And he looks exactly like the cartoon hero he is."

"You never told me that!"

She raised her brows. "Well, what did you think a Sir Morbid was, anyway?"

"I didn't think he'd be a clown!"

"Nobody's going to recognize you from that, Adam. Trust me."

He glanced back at the screen. He did have to admit that she'd cleverly changed his original features. Maybe she was right. He never looked like that. Nobody did.

"I don't know what I expected," he said in a grudging tone. "Just as long as it isn't a caricature of what you think I am."

She patted his shoulder. "I think you're just a mild-mannered architect who grumbles at every rescue he makes."

"I do *not* grumble," he grumbled.

"Of course not." She yawned, covering her open mouth with one hand. "I'm sorry. What time is it?"

"About one o'clock," he replied, suddenly realizing how pale and tired she looked. She was still wearing the heavy sweater of the night before.

She'd probably had as much sleep as he had had—almost none. "How long have you been up working on this?"

"Actually, I haven't been to bed yet," she admitted. She glanced at the clutter on the worktable and groaned. "I hate coming off a hacker's high."

"Hacker's high? What's that?" he asked suspiciously.

"Soda, candy bars, and all night hacking in front of a computer until you get the bugs out of your program," she explained. She leaned past him and began punching keys on the computer's keyboard.

"Dan does that all the time," Adam said, mildly surprised that there was actually a phrase for his brother's penchant for staying up all night with a computer.

A whirring reached his ears, and he knew from his own limited experience with the machines that she was saving her program. Good, he thought. What Diana needed now was sleep, and it looked as though he'd been elected her keeper again.

She straightened, saying, "I really ought to finish this—"

"What you need is a long nap," he interrupted. He pointed to the interior door. "Get moving."

"Since when were you elected my boss?" she demanded, her eyes narrowing.

He took her arm and steered her in the direction of the hall door. "Since now. The vote was unanimous."

"I didn't get my ballot."

"I voted for you."

"I thought this was a democracy."

"Ov course, ve haf a democracy," he said in a heavy accent. "I am democracy."

She sighed. "I'm too tired to start a revolution, commissar, but I have to reset the alarm after you leave."

"I'll reset it."

She stopped on the threshold, nearly pulling her arm out of his grip. "You don't know how to reset the alarm."

"So tell me."

She shook her head. "Sorry, there's a password. Now, if you will—Hey!"

Deciding he'd had enough of words, Adam had lifted her in his arms. She grabbed at his shoulders to steady herself.

"If I'm not allowed to reset the alarm," he said, "I'll just have to stay and guard you while you sleep. But you're going to bed now!"

"Don't treat me like a child, Adam. I'm not one, you know."

All too aware of the ripe feminine body he held, he gazed into her angry violet eyes. "Don't tempt me *not* to treat you like a child, Diana."

To his satisfaction, confusion replaced her anger. As he carried her through the house, he felt a sense of pride for holding onto his honor . . . and hers. After all, she barely knew him. He admitted, though, that it would be best to get her to her room as quickly as possible. Honor only stretched so far.

"Where's your bedroom?" he asked as he climbed the stairs.

"Second door on the right." She began to fidget. "Adam, I am capable of walking."

He grinned. "Diana, let me enjoy one rescue, at least."

She stopped squirming. "*This* is a rescue?"

"It beats the hell out of slaying dragons."

She opened her mouth in obvious protest, but a yawn emerged instead.

"No matter what I say, you're going to insist on carrying me, right?"

"Right."

She yawned again. "Okay. I know when to quit," she said as they reached the bedroom.

"Smart lady."

He gently dumped her on the bed, removed her glasses, and rolled her over on her stomach.

"What are you doing?" she demanded, trying to sit up.

Not answering, he pushed her flat on the bed while he sat on the edge. Slowly he began to knead the soft flesh of her shoulders through her sweater. As he had suspected, her muscles were tight.

"You'll go to sleep faster if you're relaxed," he said as she tensed under his hands.

She eyed him sourly over her shoulder. "Is this democracy in action again?"

"Best damn democratic dictatorship you're ever going to have."

She sighed. "I know I ought to throw you out, but I'm too tired. Besides, I have to admit the massage does feel good."

As his hands coaxed her body into relaxing completely, she sighed again and closed her eyes. She knew she really should be ordering him to stop. This was dangerous ground. But his hands were working magic on her body, and she just couldn't find the words to object to his ministrations. Languidly she stretched in counterpoint to his massaging fingers. . . .

Adam cursed silently at the innocent wantonness of her movements. He told himself she was just enjoying the massage. After all, he hadn't started it with anything more in mind than getting her to relax. And she was relaxing. He just wished she wouldn't relax in quite that way.

Gazing fixedly at her dark hair spread across the pillow, he found himself thinking of what was under the sweater and jeans. And what the sensations would be if he were massaging her soft skin. His hands would knead her back first, finding the length of her spine, and curve of her bottom. Her legs would be silk, her belly taut satin. His hands would delight in the gentle weight of her breasts. Her nipples would be swollen peaks from his kisses. . . .

An almost inaudible snore disrupted his imaginings, and Adam blinked. His hands slowing to a stop, he refocused his gaze on Diana's face. Her eyes were closed and her breathing was very even, her body completely still.

She was sound asleep.

"Damn!" he muttered in self-disgust.

He stretched out on the bed next to her and tucked his hands under his head. Diana never moved.

Staring at the ceiling, he admitted he was no ladies' man. Nonetheless, a woman had never fallen asleep on him in the bedroom before. Of course Diana had been up all night working; she was exhausted. He knew that. It wasn't exactly chivalrous to wish the princess hadn't fallen asleep so fast.

Still, that thought didn't help at all the deflated feeling he now had. Obviously his body had been expecting an entirely different ending to the massage. He smiled wryly. He'd known his honor was in trouble. Unfortunately Diana's Sleeping Beauty routine had saved it. He had to admit, though, that their relationship was moving right along. Two days, and they were already in bed together.

His smile turned into a wide grin when he heard a second soft sound from the bed's other occupant. He wondered if Diana knew she snored.

The strident ringing of a telephone penetrated Diana's deep sleep. She automatically stretched out a hand to answer it.

" 'lo?"

She dimly wondered how she could answer the telephone without actually picking up the receiver. And why was her voice two octaves lower than normal?

The sound of the receiver being replaced reached her barely functioning ears, and the strange voice said, "They hung up."

Opening her eyes, she saw that everything seemed normal.

In the next moment she realized everything was quite unnormal. Adam was in bed with her.

"What do you think you're doing?" she asked in shock, scrambling off the mattress. She stared at him as she backed away from the bed until her bottom touched the oak bureau behind her.

He stood up and ran his hands through his

obviously sleep-tousled hair. "Diana, it's okay. I'm the rescuer, remember?"

"But you were in bed with me!"

She instantly regretted the words that had accidentally slipped from her lips. She was acting like an idiot again. Surely she would have known if they had . . . if something had happened. Besides, they were both still fully dressed.

"Diana, calm down—"

"I'm calm," she interrupted, trying to pull herself together. There had to be a sophisticated way to keep the situation from becoming even more awkward. She only wished she knew what it was. She smiled, hoping her smile didn't look as shaky as it felt. "I was just surprised, that's all."

As he raised a brow, she had the feeling she wasn't fooling him in the least. She tried again. "I was just surprised you were still here."

"I wasn't about to leave you asleep all alone out here without your alarm reset. Your nearest neighbor must be at least a mile away."

"Oh, well, thank you for keeping me company, Adam." She wondered if she should thank him for the massage, then decided it wouldn't be wise for her nerves.

He began to chuckle. "Diana, if you get any more formal, you're liable to say something truly outrageous. Actually, I hadn't planned to fall asleep. It just happened. Okay?"

She hesitated, then decided it was much better to accept Adam's smoothing over of the situation than to stand there and babble.

"Okay," she agreed, while thinking it would take more than words to smooth her thudding heart and jangled nerves. Attempting to turn the conversation in another direction, she added, "You were supposed to go to Richmond today, weren't you?"

He smiled. "I can go tomorrow. Besides, it was just an excuse to see you."

She opened her mouth, then abruptly shut it as a wild notion shot through her mind. She peered at the man standing on the other side of the bed. Sleeping with a person, no matter how innocently, was an intimate act. One person didn't do intimate things unless he was attracted to the other person. From the beginning she'd been attracted to Adam, but was it possible that he really was attracted to her too?

She drew in her breath sharply at the thought.

"Diana, do I have to get down on my knees and beg forgiveness?"

His voice penetrated her numbed brain. Nervously pushing her hair off her face, she swallowed and said, "No, of course not, Adam. I was just think—ah, I guess I'm only half-awake."

He grinned at her. "I'll go get some coffee started. Or do I need a password for the machine?"

She shook her head.

"Good. I'd hate to set off an atom bomb this time."

As she watched him leave the bedroom, Diana considered her own "Adam" bomb. She knew she wasn't the type to attract men in droves. She hadn't been on a date in years! Of course, she hadn't been interested in having one, either. She'd been too busy, and she hadn't met anyone she'd been irresistibly attracted to. Until Adam.

Slowly walking around the bed to get her glasses, she wondered if she could be wrong about Adam finding her attractive. Although she hadn't seen anything in the video tape to further her original suspicions about his reasons for helping her, she knew she shouldn't just dismiss them either.

Her own judgment was no longer reliable, she thought as she put on her glasses. But surely Adam wouldn't waste much more time if he intended to make an offer from Starlight Software. Or he'd never make one. Groaning, she admitted she'd been safely locked away in her ivory tower for too long. A more sophisticated woman would know what to do about her dilemma.

She turned her head and stared at the empty bedroom doorway. A more sophisticated woman, she mused. So far she'd only been trying to show Adam that she was a mature, savvy business-woman, who couldn't be suckered into a bad deal. But a sophisticated woman would be bold and daring. A sophisticated woman would play Adam's game until she discovered the truth, one way or another. And strategy games were her business, so she ought to be a good player. Or, at least, a quick learner. Maybe it was time she stopped being Rapunzel and acquired a little sophistication. It couldn't be too hard.

On that thought, she headed for the bathroom to shower and change.

Later, dressed in a white mohair sweater and fresh jeans, she went downstairs, determined to be as sophisticated as she possibly could. When she reached the kitchen, she spotted Adam gazing out the open window at the boundaries of the verdant Tilden Regional Park. He turned and smiled at her.

"Hi."

"Hi," she said in a cracking voice. She cleared her throat.

The strong, clean aroma of brewing coffee reached her nose, and in relief she headed for the coffee maker.

"Smells great," she said, smiling at him. She poured them both a cup, managing not to spill any in spite of her suddenly awkward hands.

He walked over and picked up a cup. "Thanks."

Summoning all her courage she asked, "Can you stay for dinner?"

"I was hoping you'd ask," he said.

As she turned away, she smiled to herself. Issuing a dinner invitation was easy enough. She was positive that sophisticated women did it all the time.

Now all she had to do was figure out what came next.

Five

"How did you get started in computers, Diana?" Adam asked in between bites of salmon grilled in herb butter. "By the way, you're a terrific cook."

Seated across the glass-topped dining table from Adam, Diana immediately realized she'd been staring almost trancelike at the corded muscles of his arms. She told herself that sophisticated women probably kept a firm hold on an attraction to a man. She smiled politely at his compliment. "Thank you. To answer your question, I had a math teacher in junior high who thought I'd be good with computers and let me use the one at school."

"Obviously you were good with them," he said, grinning.

She nodded. "I'm just grateful I can make a living doing something I enjoy."

"Some of us are lucky. Now, what about men?"

"Men?" she squeaked, completely losing her slender grip on her poise. Instantly she berated herself for her lack of sophistication. She attempted a cool smile. "If you are asking me to tell you what men are, then I'm very surprised the question comes from you."

She congratulated herself on her calm answer until she saw his smile of satisfaction.

"Men do occasionally like to hear that women know what they are," he drawled. "Actually, I was asking you about any past loves."

Completely thrown by the question, she gazed at him in bewilderment. "Past loves?"

"And that answers that. Now let's go on to fantasies, hopes, and aspirations."

He wanted to know more about her, she thought, and wondered if his reason for doing so was because he was truly interested—or to find a vulnerable spot. She decided a sophisticated woman never let her vulnerability show. "My fantasy is to have Hulk Hogan carry me away to a desert island. My hope is that I have a computer with me at the time. And I aspire to live to the age of one hundred without ever catching another cold. I hate trying to breathe through a nose that feels like a squashed straw."

She grinned as Adam burst into laughter.

"Why Hulk Hogan?" he finally asked.

"Because he could move a computer without flinching. Even the portables get heavy after a while."

"Come on, now, tell the truth."

She shrugged. "There's nothing to tell, really. I've achieved my dream. I'm my own boss, and I hope it always stays that way."

She didn't say anything about her aspirations.

Right now she didn't have any, except to show Adam she wasn't a pushover.

"Don't you ever get lonely, living here by yourself?" he asked, gazing at her with an undechipherable expression.

She hesitated before answering. She didn't think she was lonely. At least she couldn't remember a time when she'd been desperate for companionship. And she wasn't a total hermit; she had her friends. "Basically I'm content."

He was silent for a moment, then said, "Most people think they're content until they have to come out of the castle. Have you come out of the castle, Diana?"

"I was never in one!" she exclaimed indignantly.

He just smiled and took another bite of salmon. "Great dinner. By the way, what's next for Sir Morbid?"

Knowing she'd been on the verge of losing her poise again, Diana was grateful for the change of subject. "Actually, Adam, your work is done as far as Sir Morbid is concerned. I told you it wouldn't take long."

"So when do I get to see this game?"

Shocked by the question, she nearly gasped aloud. Her work was top secret. Anyone's was, unless a programmer wanted it stolen. Either Adam was totally innocent about business security or he considered *her* to be totally naïve about it! Still, a sophisticated woman probably wouldn't even be surprised that he'd ask such a question. Most likely she would have been prepared for it.

Forcing a smile onto her lips, she shook her head. "I'm sorry, Adam. I make it a policy not to show my games to anyone before they're released to the public."

He smiled. To her disgust, it was a smile that told her nothing. How was she supposed to figure him out if he didn't give anything away?

"I understand," he said as he leaned back in his chair. "It's probably a sensible security measure. Not quite as exotic as barking dogs and screaming computers, though."

His voice was so bland, Diana couldn't help giggling. She was sure he'd never forget her burglar alarm.

"I'll tell you what I can do," she said as she pushed around the last of her salad with her fork. "Once I get the pictures done, I'll put them on a disk for you. What DOS are you using?"

His face went completely blank. "DOS?"

"The disk operating system on your computer. What disk operation system are you using?"

He shook his head. "I don't know what my DOS is. Actually, I didn't even know I had a DOS."

Astonished, she stared at him. Surely he knew what DOS was. Everybody involved with computers did. As the language a disk drive used to talk to a computer, DOS was nearly as basic as BASIC. And with a brother in the business, how could he not know? She decided Adam Roberts must be one heck of a spy, when he was unaware of an important part of the hardware.

"If you've got a computer, you've got a DOS," she finally said. "What's your computer?"

"BMI, but I forget which model we use," he said, shrugging.

She groaned and shook her head. "Different BMIs use different operating systems. Well, when you know what your DOS is, just give me a call and I'll take care of it."

He laughed. "That sounds nice and kinky."

She felt the heat rising to her cheeks. "What I meant was—"

He put up a hand to stop her words. "Don't. You'll spoil the image."

Realizing that any explanation would only make things worse, Diana stuffed a piece of grilled salmon in her mouth and chewed. She had to admit, though, that Adam had scored a point on the side of innocence. She just couldn't imagine a person not knowing about the tools of his business, no matter how devious his business might be.

Sophistication certainly had its pitfalls, she decided. She'd been positive she had figured out the jigsaw puzzle that was Adam Roberts. But now she was getting pieces that just didn't fit.

"It's a beautiful night. Let's sit out on the deck," Adam suggested after dinner.

A vague alarm bell rang inside Diana, but she dismissed it. What could be wrong with sitting outside on a beautiful night? And in the relaxed atmosphere she might be able to get Adam to talk even more. Maybe he'd slip up, or maybe he'd finally make the damned offer.

Or maybe she had simply gone bonkers. She had to stop using an internal scoreboard on Adam, Diana thought. Either he was guilty of acting for Starlight Software or he wasn't. The sooner she found out the answer to the puzzle, though, the better she'd feel. A little conversation out on the deck really was an excellent idea—for more than one reason.

It wasn't until after they were seated together on the old wicker settee that Diana realized her mistake. Adam was much too close. She swallowed hard, feeling her control slipping as he casually draped his arm behind her. He hadn't even touched her, yet all of her senses were spinning crazily. His jeans outlined his hard thighs, and his short-sleeved pullover was almost molded to his chest and shoulders. She could easily distinguish the scents of cologne and male in the cool night air. Her body was unnaturally tense, and her blood was beginning to throb.

She wondered what sophisticated women did in this situation, then decided they probably acted as normally as possible.

"Adam." She forced a cough to cover the croaking frog that had invaded her voice.

He turned his head. "Yes?"

Not able to think of a thing to say, she groaned silently. She was back to square one in the sophistication department. She had been better off *inside* the house.

That last thought gave her an idea, and she said, "It's a little chilly out here. Let's go back—"

"No need," he said, and brought his arm off the back of the settee to encircle her shoulders.

Before she could open her mouth to protest, he drew her against his side. She nearly moaned aloud as the heat of his body penetrated her hip and thigh. Bewilderment and anticipation swirled through her.

"Warmer?" he asked in a low voice.

Too hot, she thought as her blood seemed to

turn to molten lava. Desperately she replied, "I'm still chilly, and—"

Her words were abruptly cut off as his mouth covered hers. She tried to still her automatic response to his coaxing lips, but they teased and tantalized with soft sips at her own. His arms curved around her, pulling her closer. Then his mouth slanted across hers, melding them together.

As he deepened the kiss, sensations shot through Diana, leaving her helpless to do anything *but* respond. All her doubts and suspicions were forgotten. Her resolve crumbled at the tender demands of his lips and tongue. Her arms crept around his neck, and as they did, her hands touched bare flesh. Without hesitation she slipped her fingers beneath the collar of his shirt. His skin was warm and smooth, and she delighted in the feel of the corded muscles of his shoulders.

"So soft. So sweet," he murmured, spreading kisses down the slender column of her neck.

His hands swept under her sweater to roam across the heated skin of her back. Then his hands were between their bodies, lifting away the last barrier of her bra and caressing the hardening peaks of her breasts.

Diana couldn't breathe, couldn't think, as he teased and tormented her with the lightest of touches. Digging her nails into his shoulders, she moaned and instinctively arched her back, thrusting the full weight of her breasts into his hands.

At her electrifying reaction, Adam lost all thoughts of gentleness and finesse. He pulled her across his lap and ground his mouth into hers, seeking and finding a like response. He wanted to touch her everywhere at once, demand and take, yet give and receive. He wanted to bathe himself in her silken radiance.

He pushed her sweater and bra up until her breasts were completely unencumbered. They seemed to be made especially for his hands, and her nipples strained into his palms. Cradling her in his arms, he lowered his head and took a nipple into his mouth, tasting its velvety hardness. His mind reeled at the sensation, and her hands clutched his shoulders with sweet urgency. Her hips shifted restlessly. He smoothed a hand over them in answer. Tiny moans came from the back of her throat, entreating him to explore further.

But the moment he did, her body tensed and a hand clamped around his wrist, thrusting it away. Bewildered, he snapped his head up. Even in the darkness he could discern the confusion and panic on Diana's face, and he instantly called himself every name he could think of for his callousness.

"That was real sophisticated," she mumbled as she turned her face away and awkwardly pulled her sweater and bra back into place. She glanced at him, then looked away again. "I'm sorry."

He drew in a deep breath. Smoothing back her hair, he said gently, "You didn't do anything wrong, Diana. I did."

She whipped her head around. "Oh, no, Adam. I . . . Well, I panicked."

He covered the tensed hands in her lap with one of his. "Only because I was impatient."

She shook her head and started to speak, but he stopped her words with a tender kiss.

When he lifted his head, she sighed. "I guess you've realized I've missed out on a few things in the sex department."

He resisted smiling at her solemn tone. "You do just fine. Damn fine. And you haven't missed out on a thing. You just haven't gotten there yet."

Her shoulders shook in silent amusement. "Well, I wish I had. Then my reaction wouldn't have been so juvenile."

He squeezed her fingers. "What we need here is some experimenting in the proper manner. If you don't mind, though, since my Trans Am is a bit cramped we'll skip the heavy petting in the back seat of the car."

She burst into laughter. "Adam, you can't be serious!"

"Very. It would be like trying to do *A Chorus Line* in a taxi." He smiled at her giggles, then lifted one of her hands to his lips to kiss it. "Now, lesson number one. You always have the right to say no—at any point. I will *always* stop whenever you want me to. It is important to me that you're ready, in mind and body, rather than thinking you have to give in. Making love is give and take on both our parts."

"I'm glad one of us knows what he's doing, because I don't."

He laughed. "Oh, yes, you do. Now lesson number two . . ."

He placed her hands on his shoulders and, holding her in a loose embrace, very carefully kissed her. After a moment's hesitation she relaxed, her lips pliant and open for him to deepen the kiss. For long minutes he just kissed her. Soft, sweet kisses, their mouths moving as one with every turn and change. All the while his senses were aware of her growing desire. Her arms tightened around his neck, and she pressed her body more fully against him. He tenderly stroked her back underneath the sweater, each touch feather-light and reassuring. He was gratified when, without breaking the kiss, she shifted her body to allow him access to her breasts.

It was easier this time for him to keep his own desire under control when she moaned as he caressed her diamond-hard nipples. He kissed her cheek, her chin, the soft skin just beneath her jaw, and he could feel the racing pulse underneath. Again he pushed her sweater and bra aside and caressed the satiny globes with reverent lips and tongue until she was clawing helplessly at his shoulders. He nipped lightly at the tender flesh, then took each nipple in his mouth, suckling until she was writhing in his arms. He stroked her shoulders and back and kissed the hollow between her ribs. Ruthlessly, he suppressed his own raging desire. Then, very slowly, he let one hand drift downward, making patterns on her belly, then lower on her thighs. . . .

"Adam, please," she whispered, and moved his hand to the junction of her legs.

He raised his head and kissed her well-loved lips. "I will."

With infinite patience he deftly stroked her through her jeans. Pressing herself into his hand, she buried her face in his neck and clung. As her breath began to come in little gasps, he knew he'd completely lose control if the lesson continued. She wasn't ready to make love, he sternly told himself. Not yet. He had only wanted her to accept his touch. He forced his hand to move to her thigh, and pain knifed through him when he heard her cry of disappointment.

He held her tightly and nuzzled her throat, as his body and hers slowly relaxed. All of her was so incredibly sweet and responsive. He couldn't remember a time when he'd given so little and received so much in return.

"So that's lesson number two," she finally said, breaking into his thoughts.

He chuckled and hugged her more tightly. "Actually, I think it was lesson number twenty-seven, but we won't quibble."

She tilted her head back and looked at him. "It seems to me that you didn't have a lesson. . . . "

"Mine come later," he said, trailing kisses down her neck. He hoped the rumor about long, cold showers was true. He was definitely in need of one tonight. He ran his tongue along her delicate collarbone and added, "You were magnificent."

Her arms tightened around his shoulders. "I had a magnificent teacher."

He smothered a sigh. He wasn't sure if he liked her thinking of him as a "teacher." Teaching implied that one learned and eventually graduated. More and more he was realizing how precious Diana was, how refreshingly different from other women. He'd be crazy if he let her slip away.

He decided that, before too much more time passed, he'd better insure that Diana stayed in class for a long time.

A very long time.

Waking to thoughts of Adam and the night before, Diana stretched lazily and rolled over onto her side, away from the bright sunshine, which bathed her bedroom in a golden glow. She wasn't ready to begin her working day just yet. Besides, she didn't want to look at pictures of Sir Morbid, when she could daydream about the real man under the armor.

She smiled, deciding her sophisticated attitude the night before really had paid off. Last night had proved that Adam couldn't be involved in some business plot regarding her. If he were, he surely would have made a physical conquest as an added victory. She knew she never would have stopped him a second time. But he'd been so caring and understanding, when she'd been . . . fragile. Not many men would have been that patient with her, she guessed, or even would have cared about her inexperience. She chuckled, thinking that she'd always known Adam had all the qualities of a chivalrous knight. *She* certainly felt like a princess who'd just been rescued from some terrible fate.

He had taken her to heights she'd never imagined. Even now she could feel the melting in her veins. She knew, though, that she'd only tasted what making love with Adam would be like. Although he hadn't truly known it, he had been right about her missing out on that teenage rite, parking. She'd been in very few back seats of cars during her high-school years. At the time, she'd only been curious to see if all the hoopla about boys had merit. It hadn't. Her few dates hadn't been exactly overeager either. In college she'd come to the conclusion that some people had relationships and some people didn't, and that she was in the second category. She'd never been disappointed, or thought it was something inside her that needed fixing. She'd always been too involved with her work to do more than briefly wonder about her lack of libido. Of course she'd never realized she could be a late bloomer. A very late bloomer.

She'd missed out on quite a bit, she thought, and had quite a bit to learn. But better late than never.

The telephone rang, interrupting her thoughts. Smiling, she languidly stretched out her arm to answer it.

"Hello," she said in a soft voice.

The telephone clicked, and all she heard was the dial tone.

Diana frowned, remembering the call that had awakened her and Adam yesterday. That had been a hang-up too. She wondered if she were about to be subjected to a series of annoying prank calls from kids who had discovered her number.

The telephone rang again.

Picking up the receiver, she said hesitantly, "Hello?"

"Hi. It's me."

She instantly recognized the whiskey-low voice of her cousin Angelica, and figured there had been a bad connection the first time. She suppressed a stab of disappointment that the caller wasn't Adam.

"You sound like you're still in bed, kid," Angelica said. "Been on another all-night binge?"

Diana laughed as she fluffed the pillow behind her. Angelica was seven months younger than she, and yet always called her "kid." "A different kind of binge, Angelica, only not all night."

"Now, that sounds interesting."

"You're beginning to pry," Diana said.

"I beg to differ with you. I am only concerned

for a close and treasured relative. Now that I've managed a properly righteous tone of indignation—tell me all the juicy details. He must be spectacular to pull you away from your computers!"

"What makes you think it's a man?" Diana asked suspiciously.

"You are out of your league, kid, if you think you can smooth that kind of thing past me. Unless, of course, you want to."

"I want to. Are you angry?"

Angelica laughed. "Of course not. I'm your friend. Besides, I know how it is when a woman wants to keep a terrific man to herself. You'll tell me when you want to, and then you'll have a lot more to tell."

Diana had a fit of giggles at her cousin's logic. Angelica always had been sneaky.

"I'm glad to see you're in a good mood this morning," Angelica continued. "Because I'm in a puzzled one. I got a phone call just now from Starlight Software."

Diana shot up in the bed, her fingers forming a death grip on the phone. No, she thought wildly. No! Swallowing back the knot in her throat, she said, "And?"

"And it wasn't from that high-and-mighty jerk of an acquisitions manager whom I dealt with the last time. It was from Dan Roberts, the owner. He made another offer for your games, Diana. And it was exactly the same as their last offer."

"And what did you say?" Diana was afraid to ask anything else, afraid even to think of the implications of Starlight's offer.

"Naturally, I said that it was unacceptable to my client. You know that we have several standing offers from other software houses that are much more generous than Starlight's."

Her stomach sinking to the floor, Diana asked, "And what did Roberts say?"

"He kept insisting that *you* be told about the offer. If I didn't know better, I'd say he sounded like a man who had already sewed up a deal and was just going through the motions for etiquette's sake. Very confident, and almost smug. That's what's so puzzling. Do you have any idea why he'd think that?"

"Not a clue," Diana answered without hesitation, all the while feeling as if she'd just taken first prize in an idiot contest. But she'd be damned before she'd tell her cousin that.

"Then I'll call him back and tell him, 'No, thanks.' "

Diana opened her mouth to say, "Damn straight!" then shut it. Something inside her balked at an outright refusal.

"Let's wait a bit on a final no, Angelica," she said slowly, following her instincts.

"But why?"

"Well . . . I'm a bit puzzled, too, that he's so confident. Even though the computer industry is close-knit and we're both 'third-generation hackers,' I've never met Dan Roberts but I have heard of him." She smiled bitterly. "Fortunately, I do happen to have a line of communication into Starlight, so I think I'll do some digging and see what they're up to. In the meantime, just tell him I'm thinking it over."

"Are you sure?"

"Quite sure. I'll talk to you later, Angelica."

Diana hung up the receiver and stared blindly

at the flowered wallpaper opposite her bed. Pain washed through her.

So the offer had finally come, she thought. She couldn't believe it, just couldn't believe it after last night. Especially after last night. That rat . . . that creep . . . that . . . that . . .

She searched her mind for a word that best suited Adam Roberts, but gave up in frustration at her limited vocabulary of curses. While she might have made the first move with Adam, he and his brother had certainly taken advantage of it. Thinking it over, she realized that their maneuvering had been diabolically simple. Adam was to work the personal angle with her. Once he'd firmly established himself in her life—very innocently, of course—Dan would again bid for her games. Naturally, how could she refuse when she was involved with Adam?

Pounding her fists on the mattress, she forced herself to ignore the stinging tears behind her eyes. She'd never in her life shed tears over a man, and she wouldn't start now. Bitter as it was to swallow, she knew she had nobody to blame but herself. Even though she had seen the warning signs in the beginning, even though she'd had her suspicions all along, Adam had still managed to play her for a fool. She'd allowed her body to do the thinking instead of her brain.

He'd made one little mistake, though, she thought. He hadn't insured that she was totally wrapped around his finger before they'd made the offer. Thank goodness she'd only gotten to lesson twenty-seven! Otherwise her humiliation would have been unbearable.

Straightening, she muttered with satisfaction, "Now let them stew."

The brothers would probably go crazy, wondering if they'd succeeded with her or not. She liked that. She suspected, too, that Adam wouldn't just disappear now. After all, the game wasn't quite played out. Most likely he would be even more visible, and more persuasive, until her signature was on the contract. But he'd controlled the game too long.

Now it was her turn. And she was a games master.

"Welcome to the real world, Rapunzel," she told herself as she scrambled out of bed.

She decided the first step was a bit of pride-rescuing. It was about time she started rescuing herself anyway. Meanwhile, she'd better start hanging around the docks. Her vocabulary really did need a brush-up.

Six

Driving her Datsun Z-80 through the busy streets of Oakland, Diana smiled her first genuine smile of the day.

She had the beginnings of a plan.

As she parked her car in the four-storied parking garage downtown, she decided her plan was a simple one too. And as she walked into the suite of offices containing Adam's architectural firm, she congratulated herself for implementing the first step of the plan with barely a nervous flutter of her pulse.

But when Adam's receptionist told her he wouldn't be in until later in the afternoon, Diana felt her shoulders sag in surprising relief.

Maybe she wasn't quite as ready to implement the plan as she'd first thought.

Then she straightened her shoulders. She'd completely forgotten that Adam had said he had to check on a site in Richmond today, but she couldn't quit now just because she'd made a little mistake. Clearing her throat, she smiled at the well-dressed young woman seated on the other side of the desk and asked, "Would it be possible to leave a message for Mr. Roberts?"

"Sure," the receptionist replied, picking up a pen. Diana gazed at the cinnamon-red polish on the woman's very long nails as she attempted to form a personal yet neutral message.

Finally she said, "Just tell him Diana Windsor stopped by, and she'll be having a drink at the— the Oakland Towers Hotel around . . . six this evening, if he'd like to join her."

The receptionist smiled as she wrote down the message. "He ought to be back at about half-past three. In the meantime, is there somewhere he can reach you, should he call in?"

"No. I'll be . . . shopping."

The receptionist nodded. Diana said good-bye and walked away. She tried not to walk too fast. Running was ridiculous, she thought, as she forced her feet to keep a sedate pace. Besides, one part of her plan called for some more sophistication, and it surely wasn't sophisticated to run like a scared kid.

Somehow she managed to maintain her composure until she reached the sidewalk. Instantly she sprinted away from the tall office building, mumbling apologies when she bumped into several pedestrians. She was three long city blocks from Adam's office before she slowed to a stop.

This was getting her nowhere fast, she thought, and firmly reminded herself that she shouldn't be afraid or embarrassed to face Adam again. The shame was *his* for what he had done. She had every right to string him, and his brother, along, every right to act sweet and almost love-sick until Adam was bragging to his brother that she was signed, sealed, and delivered. And then she had every right to turn around and sell her game wherever she darn well pleased.

Never get angry, she told herself with smug satisfaction, just get even.

Glancing at her watch, she moaned when she realized it would be nearly five hours before her drink with Adam—if he showed up. She dismissed the doubt. He'd show up. Under the circumstances, he probably wouldn't be able to stay away.

She grinned. If he thought she would mention the offer from Starlight Software to him, he'd better think again.

Still, it would be long hours before they were to meet, and she wondered if she should go back home. She didn't want to fight the traffic, but she had no idea how to fill the time. Then she chuckled to herself. She'd told the receptionist she'd be shopping.

So she'd go shopping.

A little before six that evening Diana walked into the Oakland Towers' lobby. Immediately she spotted Adam already waiting by the elevators. In his gray pinstripe suit, he looked like a no-nonsense but very virile business executive. She remembered his sensual tutoring of the night before in a rush of sensations. And she remembered his betrayal of the morning. Her steps faltered and she fought the urge to turn around and run. Drawing a deep breath, she steeled herself to face him, when he caught sight of her and waved. He hurried over.

"Hello, Adam," she said as he drew near her. She gave silent thanks that she actually sounded normal. Her stomach was churning, her chest was heaving, and her body was unnaturally stiff. She couldn't believe her physical reaction to him was stronger than ever, especially after the morning's revelation.

"Hi," he said softly. "I'm sorry I missed you earlier at the office. I really would like to have shown you around."

She forced herself to smile. "I would have enjoyed that."

His voice grew deep. "I wanted to call you this morning—"

"I'm almost glad you didn't," she broke in, her own voice low. She edged away from him as unobtrusively as possible. "I wanted to surprise you by taking you to lunch. Unfortunately, I forgot you had to go to Richmond on business."

She sighed silently, grateful there had been no betraying awkwardness on her part. Somehow, she hadn't panicked, and had even managed to sound almost flirty. The worst had to be over now. She hoped.

Adam gazed at Diana's lush mouth. He wanted to kiss her, to carry her away and finish the lesson of the night before. He wanted to ignore his honor, but couldn't. Diana needed time. If only her mouth didn't look so soft and moist. Suddenly he noticed she was wearing lipstick . . . and eye shadow. And a sweater that outlined her magnificent breasts. Diana had always seemed like an

Eve to him—natural, innocent, and earthy. So why . . . ?

He hid a grin, realizing she had dressed up, put on makeup, for him. There was no need. She was fine to begin with. Still, he had to admit he liked the enhancements. . . .

As he continued to stare at her mouth, Diana nearly did panic. Was her pale pink lipstick crooked? Too heavy? Downright clownish? She prayed it wasn't. The lipstick had looked okay in the bright lights of the department store's ladies' room. So had the mascara and light blue eye shadow she'd applied. In fact, they had looked barely there. Maybe the makeup clashed with the pretty silver-and-blue designer sweater she'd purchased. She'd only wanted to look a little more sophisticated, not ridiculous.

"I like that sweater," Adam said, slipping his arm around her waist. "Shall we go have a drink now?"

She nodded, relaxing at the obvious sincerity in his voice. Evidently her little impromptu changes were having the desired effect. She decided her plan was moving along quite nicely, despite her initial setback. All she had to do was keep a layer of detachment between herself and Adam. Easier said than done, she admitted as his arm seemed to burn her waist.

As they walked to the elevators she congratulated herself on her choice of meeting place. The restaurant and bar were on the top floor of the hotel, overlooking Lake Merritt. If nothing else, they could talk about the terrific view.

The elevator doors opened and they stepped inside. As she turned around to face forward, Diana almost gasped out loud as the most beautiful woman she'd ever seen rushed into the elevator just as the doors were closing. Light perfume filled the enclosed space. Diana completely forgot about Adam.

"Morgan's going to kill me," the woman muttered as she pushed the already lighted button for the restaurant.

Diana stared at the redhead's pale yellow cocktail dress. Obviously expensive, the long-sleeved dress clung to the woman's body as if it had been designed for it. Probably it had. It was barely held together by gold clasps at the shoulders, and the neckline draped impossibly low, exposing much of the woman's cleavage. As Diana's gaze drifted upward to the expertly made-up face, she noted that in spite of her comment, the woman looked gorgeous, confident, and . . . sophisticated.

"That's a beautiful dress," Diana said to the woman. Normally she didn't speak to people in elevators, but she just had to tell the woman how much she liked the dress.

The woman turned and smiled, pleasure evident in her brown eyes. "Thank you. I hope my husband has the same reaction. Maybe then he won't strangle me for being so late. The traffic over the Bay Bridge was terrible! That's a pretty sweater you're wearing. I love those silver snowflake appliqués."

Diana thanked her, and decided that whoever the woman was, she was very nice. Then she became aware of Adam again and realized he hadn't spoken a word since they'd entered the elevator. She glanced up to find him staring almost open-mouthed at the woman. She shifted her gaze back to the woman. She could understand Adam's staring. After all, her own reaction had been the same. But was he attracted to her?

She stiffened at the thought. The doors opened just then, and Adam suddenly came to life, whisking them both through the doors. Finally, he acknowledged the woman with a rather curt nod of his head.

The woman smiled politely at him, then said to Diana, "It was nice of you to defy the elevator code of silence and speak to me. Those were probably the last kind words I'll hear for the rest of the evening. Speaking of evenings, have a nice one yourselves. The hotel's restaurant is supposed to be very good." The woman's smile turned into a mischievous grin. "Well, I'm off to make a grand entrance. My husband never has learned to cope with one of those."

The woman hurried away in the direction of a private reception room, and as she watched her go, Diana couldn't imagine the woman's husband even having the ability to speak after seeing that dress. Adam certainly hadn't. It was even more depressing to admit that *she* hadn't left him silently gawking as the redhead had.

She forced a smile to her lips. She wasn't about to let him know that his reaction to the woman had upset her in the least. "She was very beautiful, wasn't she?"

Adam grinned. "Yes, she was. But I know good fortune when I find it, princess."

More than good fortune, he thought as he smoothed his hand down the length of her spine.

Diana, with her huge violet eyes and sexy naïveté, was much more beautiful than the redhead. He'd never had a woman obviously make herself look prettier because she thought it would please him. Diana had also given over a measure of trust to him last night, and he had never felt so honored in his life. Now he had to protect that vulnerable trust, nurture it. And he would. Women like Diana came along only once in a man's lifetime—if they ever did. And if a man was very lucky, he'd recognize her. He *was* a very lucky man.

On that thought, he ushered her into the Tropical Room. The decor was overdone with bamboo and palm fronds. Even the waitresses' sarong uniforms looked hokey to Adam. But the place had a certain thirties-era charm.

They were seated in tall fanback chairs by one of the panoramic windows and ordered drinks. Adam watched in amusement as Diana kept fiddling with the zipper on her purse. After a minute she asked, "How was Richmond?"

"Very good. We're doing the renovations for several commercial properties, and the construction is just about ready to start. Between the massive redevelopment projects here in Oakland and there, my partner, John Polaski, and I figure we won't be out of work for the next hundred years or so."

"That's wonderful!" she exclaimed. "When did you start your business?"

"About three years ago." He grinned lopsidedly. "Like you, I prefer working for myself, even though I work harder. But it's worth it."

She nodded. Suddenly she leaned forward, staring directly into his eyes. "You know, I never asked you . . . but are you married?"

He burst into laughter.

Diana felt a hot blush cover her cheeks. Really, she thought. He didn't have to laugh quite that loud. Maybe the question wasn't exactly subtle, but it had suddenly occurred to her that she ought to know. Now she wished she'd never asked.

"I just thought I'd check, that's all," she said in a rush, trying to cover her embarrassment. "I mean . . . you never said . . . I never knew . . ." She collapsed back in the chair and began to laugh. "It was a heck of a question, wasn't it?"

"It sure was," he agreed. "And no, I'm not married. Never even came close."

"Why?" she asked, curious.

He shrugged. "Just never found the right woman. Why aren't you married?"

She shrugged. "Too busy, I guess."

"Same here."

Grinning, she said, "Taking a page from your book, what about fantasies, hopes, and aspirations?"

He grinned back. "My fantasies couldn't get much better than last night. My hope is that there will be more nights like that. My aspiration is to figure out how to change the oil in my car without getting the stuff all over me."

She laughed at the last. She refused to think about the first two. "Are you originally from here?" she asked in an attempt to change the subject.

He shook his head. "Seattle. My family is still there. I moved here about five years ago to work for a big architectural firm. Then John and I struck out on our own."

She couldn't have asked for a better opening.

"Oh!" she said very innocently. "Seattle is where your brother's software company is. Starbright, right?"

"Starlight," he corrected her in an amused voice. "We sound like we're rhyming sentences."

"I have to admit I'm a little curious about your brother, seeing as we're in the same line of work. Has his company been in business long?"

Before Adam could answer, a waitress, different from the one who had taken their order, arrived with their drinks. A very attractive waitress with blond streaks in her dark, windblown-styled hair. She bent especially low when she placed Adam's Scotch and water on the wicker table. Diana couldn't see the waitress's face, but somehow the woman's whole body seemed to exude sexual invitation.

Feeling like a struggling rookie surrounded by superstars, Diana glanced down at her sweater and old navy skirt. The silver snowflakes that had distinguished the sweater from the others on the rack now looked childish, and to her critical eyes the skirt showed its age. Her navy pumps, with their short, squat heels, were so damned sensible too.

The waitress left with a last swish of her sarong. Diana cringed, wondering how she could have been so stupid as to think her own appearance was the least sophisticated or womanly. Her attention had been focused on the waitress, but she could well imagine Adam's expression as he'd received a close-up view of the low-cut sarong. She grabbed her glass of white wine and took a large gulp of the tangy liquid.

"I foresee another rescue in the works if you keep drinking like that," Adam said gently.

She carefully set the glass back down on the table. First the redhead, then the waitress, and now this! She sighed and absently adjusted her glasses on the bridge of her nose. She had a long way to go before she'd be a master in the game of sophistication. There were mazes and obstacles that she just hadn't anticipated. Still, she did have one advantage, for which she was very grateful. She knew exactly what Adam's game was. And that, she decided, made them just about even.

"Diana?"

She raised her head and looked at Adam, at his tender expression. He really was quite good at faking it, she thought.

"I get the feeling something's bothering you," he continued, leaning forward. "If it's last night, then I think we should talk."

Frantically she searched for an adroit way to turn the topic of conversation to something neutral. Of all the darned times to be out of sophistication! Swallowing back a lump of desperation, she said, "I'm not uncomfortable about . . . anything, Adam. I did some shopping this afternoon, and I'm a little tired from that. That's probably what you're noticing."

He frowned at her, and Diana knew she hadn't fooled him. Her heart pounding, she forced herself to say, "Last night was just . . . last night. There's really nothing to discuss. And especially not *here*."

"There's plenty to discuss," he countered. "But you're right about not here. Finish your drink, and we'll go to my place—"

"Honestly, I'm fine," she broke in, horrified by his suggestion. "Quite happy, in fact. Brimming with a healthy attitude about private lessons, thanks to you—"

"Well, well. If it isn't Princess Di and her body-guard."

Startled by the unexpected interruption, Diana glanced up to discover Jim Griegson standing next to their table, a drink in his hand. From the glazed look in his eyes and the sour smile playing on his lips, she had the feeling this drink wasn't his first of the evening. She nearly groaned aloud when she remembered the last time she'd seen the *CompuWorld* reporter—and his boardroom/bedroom comment in his last column. She only hoped he had calmed down about Adam's having pushed him into the buffet table. While Jim was the last person she might want to see, she did have to admit that his appearance was very timely. She'd been babbling herself into disaster.

"This is a private conversation," Adam said curtly.

"I see you're still the great protector, Roberts," Griegson said in a sarcastic voice.

"I'm really sorry about what happened at the reception, Jim," Diana said, feeling that if she didn't dispel the thick tension between the two men, there would be another disaster. "And so is Adam. Why don't you join us? We owe you amends."

"No, thanks," Griegson said, then smirked. "I wouldn't lower myself to hoist one with the *Virgin* Queen and her consort."

Before Diana could even be shocked by the crude words, Adam exploded out of his chair. Griegson yelped in fright, and jumped away from the fist that never materialized. He crashed into the bamboo furniture behind him and went down in a tangle of legs, table, and chairs.

Diana blinked once in amazement.

"You owe the *lady* an apology," Adam said in a cold voice, standing over the dazed reporter.

Realizing that Jim was too stunned to apologize for anything, Diana rose unsteadily to her feet. The other patrons were staring in shock. She still found it hard to believe that Jim had been insulting both her and Adam one moment, and was sprawled on the floor the next. Touching Adam's arm to get his attention, she said quietly, "I do believe you've delivered our usual exit signal, Adam."

He turned, a furious expression still on his face, then visibly relaxed. With a last disparaging glance at Griegson, he reached into his pocket and pulled out a handful of bills. Tossing them on the table, he said to Diana, "Time to go."

"No kidding," she muttered as he took her elbow. "You shouldn't have scared him like that, Adam. Jim was just drunk, and his pride was probably bruised from what happened the last time."

"Too bad," Adam said, guiding her away from the wreckage. "Anyway, the guy needed a quick lesson in chivalry. I don't suppose you'd like to try for dinner in the restaurant," he added wryly.

"After what you just paid for the drinks, I don't think you can afford the price of dinner."

A bartender suddenly stood in their path. With an overwhelming sense of déjà vu, Diana rolled her eyes heavenward and muttered under her breath, "Happens every time." More loudly she said, "I'm terribly sorry about the mess, sir. My friend, here, was just showing me how he knocked out his opponent and won the bronze medal at the . . . Vienna Olympics. Unfortunately, that poor man was passing by during the instant replay. It was a terrible mistake, and we're sorry for any inconvenience it might have caused to your beautiful establishment."

"Real sorry, Mac," Adam said, and Diana forced herself not to react to his suddenly acquired Brooklyn accent.

"I believe," she added, "you'll find more than adequate compensation on the table."

"Just as long as you're goin' and not comin' back," the bartender said.

Grateful that he was letting them off without more fuss, Diana nodded and slipped around him. Adam was right behind her.

"Thanks for the rescue," he whispered in her ear when they reached the elevators.

"I owed you one," she said, smiling at him.

She couldn't help feeling that he really did have a streak of honor, despite the sneaky trick he was pulling on her. He had certainly rushed in to defend her against Jim's nasty remark.

The elevator arrived, and to her surprise Adam began to laugh as soon as they'd stepped inside and the elevator started down to the lobby.

"Vienna Olympics!" he gasped out as she stared at him in puzzlement.

"What was wrong with Vienna Olympics?" she asked.

"The Olympics have never been in Vienna, Diana."

America's most popular, most compelling romance novels...

Here, at last...love stories that really involve you!
Fresh, finely crafted novels with story lines so
believable you'll feel you're actually living them!
Characters you can relate to...exciting places to
visit...unexpected plot twists...all in all, exciting
romances that satisfy your mind and delight
your heart.

EXAMINE 4 LOVESWEPT NOVELS FOR

15 Days FREE!

To introduce you to this fabulous service, you'll get four brand-
new Loveswept releases not yet in the bookstores. These four
exciting new titles are yours to examine for 15 days without
obligation to buy. Keep them if you wish for just $9.95 plus
postage and handling and any applicable sales tax.

☐ **YES,** please send me four new romances for a 15-day
FREE examination. If I keep them, I will pay just $9.95 plus
postage and handling and any applicable sales tax and you will
enter my name on your preferred customer list to receive all four
new Loveswept novels published each month *before* they are
released to the bookstores—always on the same 15-day free
examination basis.

20123

Name_____

Address_____

City_____

State_____ Zip_____

My Guarantee: I am never required to buy any shipment unless I
wish. I may preview each shipment for 15 days. If I don't want it, I
simply return the shipment within 15 days and owe nothing for it.

R 1

Now you can be sure you'll never, ever miss a single Loveswept title by enrolling in our special reader's home delivery service. A service that will bring all four new Loveswept romances published every month into your home—and deliver them to you before they appear in the bookstores!

Examine 4 Loveswept Novels for

15 days FREE!

(SEE OTHER SIDE FOR DETAILS)

She groaned. "I hope the bartender didn't know that."

"He probably did, but he was too glad to see our backsides heading out the door to call you a liar." He patted her bottom, then leaned over and kissed her on the mouth. "And a beautiful backside you've got, too."

She felt the heat rising to her cheeks and resisted the urge to pat his backside in return.

Seven

"Are you sure you won't stay in town and have dinner, Diana?"

Even as he asked the question, Adam already knew the answer.

Diana was looking across the roof of her car to the pink and orange streaks of the sunset. Then her gaze returned to his, and he could easily read the wistful expression in her eyes.

"Much as I would like to, I should be going," she said. "I hope you don't mind."

He did, but he knew it was probably for the best. After the near-brawl with Griegson, he didn't trust his honor. Half of him wanted to wipe away the reporter's insult by gently making love to her. The other half wanted to make love to her, too, but as a primitive claim of his rights as protector. Unfortunately, he knew that Diana's emotions were confused at the moment. He'd realized it when she'd insisted on returning to the garage where her car was parked, as soon as they'd reached the lobby of the hotel. Too much had happened too fast, and, frustrating as it was, if he wasn't careful he could very easily drive her away. But with a little patience and gentle courtship, he'd have Diana.

"I'll only excuse you tonight if you'll have dinner with me tomorrow night," he said, deciding he had the right to exert one small claim. After all, one could reap a fortune with a series of small claims just as well as with one big strike.

"Do you think we might be heading for another rescue?" she asked, grinning.

He laughed. "I'm beginning to have a real soft spot for rescues. But if we are, between us we might just manage to get through it. Want to take a chance?"

She hesitated for a moment, then nodded. "I'm an adventurous soul. How about at Solomon Grundy's in Berkeley? That way we can split the driving and meet there."

He frowned, knowing she was avoiding having him pick her up at her house—and possibly not leaving afterward. Still, it was a small concession to allow her control over dinner. "Fine. Eight o'clock?"

She nodded again. He leaned forward and touched his mouth to hers. Tenderly, he played at her lips, feeling them grow pliant. But he didn't deepen the kiss. Instead he indulged in a series of gentle caresses, each one longer than the last, until he heard her soft, helpless sounds of surrender.

He lifted his head and smiled as she opened glazed eyes. Nudging her to one side, he took her keys, then unlocked her car and helped her into the driver's seat. He smothered a chuckle at the confused expression on her face.

"Be careful on the way home," he said. He gave her a hard kiss on her love-swollen mouth, then shut the car door and waved good-bye.

"Dammit!" Adam exclaimed, angrily swiping a hand through his hair. "The hotel management already approved those designs for the annex!"

John Polaski shook his head. "I know. But with the convention center less than two blocks away, they're still afraid they're underestimating future business."

"But we've changed those designs once before for space reasons. We just can't squeeze any more out of the site without going to a second floor, and those idiots refuse to do that because 'it might hamper the view' of Lake Merritt."

"We can't cut down on sidewalk space, either, without violating city ordinances," John said, studying the blueprints lying on the drafting table.

"And if that's what the hotel wants, they can take their annex elsewhere," Adam grumbled, staring over John's shoulder at the blueprints. "Damn thing looks like a box with holes in it."

John chuckled. "An architect should never grouse about his own designs. Any ideas on how to keep the clients happy? And fast?"

"No, but I'd be happy to tell them where to stuff their annex—and fast. Lord, what a mess." He slammed his hand on the table. "Damn! I don't suppose this can wait until tomorrow, can it?"

John cleared his throat. "If we can afford their blaming us for missed construction deadlines . . ."

"We can't," Adam said flatly.

He strode over to his sleek, modern desk chair and sat down. Leaning back, he rubbed his temples and tried not to think of having to cancel his dinner with Diana. Instead he concentrated on the problem of fitting a large restaurant, private banquet rooms, and a shopping mall into the space of a telephone booth. At least if he came up with a decent idea to present to the hotel management this afternoon, he might be able to make dinner that evening.

He groaned. Even if he managed to think of something, he'd still have to redo the designs. He doubted the hotel would be sympathetic about a dinner date. Hell, he thought. Solomon Grundy's had great cuisine, and it overlooked the bay. . . .

An idea popped into his head, and he sat up. "John! What about putting the restaurant and reception rooms on the roof?"

"They're adamant about no second floor—"

"With gardens, John. A rooftop garden restaurant, completely glass-enclosed. The mall itself could then take up the whole first floor. The restaurant could be larger, yet there still would be some open space. With a great view of the lake—and a little convincing on our part that the hotel patrons wouldn't be able to resist dining in such beautiful surroundings—I think the hotel might go for it."

John rubbed his ear for a moment. "They just might."

"Good. Do me a favor, John. Call them and set up a meeting. I'll get started on some rough sketches—very rough ones. Be sure to add that, please." He gave his partner a crooked grin. "I hope they're smart enough to realize they're going to be billed all over again for this."

"If they ain't, they soon will be," John said, and slipped through the door connecting their offices.

As soon as the door closed, Adam reached for the telephone to call Diana. But just as his fingers touched the receiver, the phone rang. Surprised, he lifted the receiver to his ear and said hello.

"Adam? It's Dan. I can only spare a moment, but I wanted to let you know I'll be in San Francisco Thursday and Friday on business. Can we get together for dinner?"

Adam grinned. "I can spare a moment to say yes."

"Great! I'll call you when I get in and we can pick a spot, okay?"

"Fine." An image of Diana flitted through his mind, and Adam's grin widened. "Can I bring a friend?"

"Well . . . Sure, I guess, if you want to."

"You don't sound very enthusiastic about meeting Diana Windsor."

There was complete silence on the other end of the telephone.

"Dan? Are you there?"

"I think there was something wrong with the phone just then," Dan finally said. "Did you say Diana Windsor?"

"Yep. You have any objections to that?"

"No, no!" Dan sounded stunned. "Actually, I'd love to meet her. But I thought you were only helping her with her game."

"I did." Adam stifled a laugh at taking his brother by surprise. "Anyway, I know she'd like to meet you. Strictly personal, though, Daniel. And very personal to me. No business."

"Oh . . . ah . . . yes, of course. Adam, is there something going on between you and her?"

"Something. Listen, I won't keep you. Besides, I'm swamped with work too. Take care, Dan, and call me when you get in. 'Bye."

He broke the connection before his brother could say his farewells, then called Diana. He was just about to hang up on the twelfth ring when she finally answered.

He heard a faint "Damn! I forgot the answering machine again," then, louder, "Hello?"

"Hello. This is Adam, a human being who hates to talk to answering machines."

"Oh! Adam. I'm sorry—"

"I'm the one who's sorry," he interrupted gently, "but I'm afraid I can't make dinner tonight. A hotel we're designing an annex for just delivered us a disaster. Can we change it to Thursday or Friday?"

"Well . . . ah . . . ."

He chuckled. "Now you sound like my brother. Actually, that's why I'd like to know if you'll be free either of those nights. He'll be in town then, and I would really like you to meet Dan. I know he'd like to meet you."

"I see." There was a long pause, and Adam began to wonder if his phone was broken. At last, her voice came back on the line. "I'm free either of those nights. I think it would be very . . . appropriate to meet your brother, don't you?"

He frowned at the stilted coolness of her voice. "Diana, if you don't want to have dinner with Dan, just say so. I won't be hurt."

"Oh, no, Adam. Actually, I'd . . . love to meet your brother. In fact, I wouldn't miss it for the world. But I don't want to intrude. I'm sure you two have a lot to talk about."

"You're never an intrusion. . . ."

When he hung up shortly afterward, Adam couldn't help grinning. Diana and his brother ought to get along just fine.

Diana hung up the phone and stared at it thoughtfully.

After the confrontation with Jim Griegson yesterday, she'd had enough of her plan. Each time she had thought she'd been starting to make a little progress, she'd run into some unseen barrier. So she'd retreated to her "tower," knowing she just wouldn't be capable of handling dinner with Adam, too, that night.

Smiling wryly, she acknowledged that mostly she'd been terrified by the thought of what might happen after dinner. Once fed, her body seemed to have a mind of its own. She'd suspected she'd never be able to withstand another lesson, and had known for sure when he'd kissed her good-bye. She'd felt as if she were standing dangerously close to the edge of a deep precipice, and if she weren't extremely careful she'd tumble in. A twenty-four-hour respite before facing Adam again had seemed very sensible.

But by agreeing to have dinner with the *brothers* Roberts, she'd moved her plan ahead several stages. Several major stages.

She grimaced, deciding it was more like having dinner with the brothers Knife-in-the-Back. Envisioning herself sitting between two male vipers, she wondered how she would ever be able to swallow a morsel of food. The opportunity to play them for a couple of suckers, though, was just too tempting to pass up. Still, the situation would require a healthy blending of confidence and sophistication.

"Of which you have scored zippo," she reminded herself tartly.

If only she had more time, she thought. But it was like being a novice game-player again, with her back against a great locked door, the nasties moving in for the kill, and no key to be had anywhere. The solution usually entailed figuring out some way of taking the nasties by surprise, then outsmarting them. She felt she could handle the outsmarting part, but Adam, unfortunately, had always managed to surprise her. Somehow she had to surprise him, and she needed the weapons with which to do it.

Remembering how out of place she'd felt yesterday among more experienced women, she groaned aloud. Without the right tools she'd feel—and look—just as inadequate as ever. . . .

Diana blinked.

The woman in the elevator had *looked* sophisticated and confident. The waitress had *looked* sexy.

"That's the key!" she exclaimed, shaking her fists in triumph.

She'd wanted to acquire sophistication, thinking she'd be more confident and better able to handle Adam. She'd been heading in the right direction yesterday, with her little attempts at enhancing her attractiveness to him, but they hadn't been drastic enough. And she hadn't considered matching the inner Diana to the outer one.

If she looked really sophisticated and confident, it was only logical that she'd really feel sophisticated and confident. And it wouldn't hurt matters if she threw in a bit of sexiness too.

She grinned. Adam wouldn't know what hit him.

Her grin faded when she realized she had very little knowledge of makeup, hairstyles, or fashion. Then she remembered the light blond streaks in the waitress's dark hair. They had certainly looked dramatic. And sexy. Might as well start from the top and work down one step at a time, she decided.

The first step in her new plan called for a trip to the local drugstore.

Three hours later Diana stood in front of her bathroom mirror. She'd purchased a premixed hair-streaking kit and had avoided judging the probable result while she'd been applying the solution. She'd wanted to surprise herself with the finished effect. She hadn't even given in to the temptation to peek after the last rinse. Instead she'd wrapped a towel around her head, turban-style. Very carefully she now removed the towel, put on her glasses, and stared at her brand-new image.

She screamed in horror.

Her hair was white! Completely white on top, with big gobs of black underneath. In disbelief she reached up and touched the damp straw disaster she'd created. It was all too real. Maybe it would look better when it was combed out, she thought wildly, her fingers scrambling for the comb.

Tears of frustration and despair welled in her eyes at the resulting vanilla-fudge mass. No doubt about it, she looked like a zombie from a bad B movie.

Adam would be stunned speechless, all right, she thought. And after that, he'd be laughing hysterically.

With shaking hands she picked up the directions and read them once more, this time in hopes that she'd missed something. She hadn't. Yet somehow she'd totally botched it.

Her telephone rang. Panic-stricken, she whirled around and stared through the doorway into her bedroom.

She wouldn't answer it, she decided. It might be Adam, and she just knew he'd be rolling on the floor in hysterics at her hair. . . .

"Don't be ridiculous!" she sternly told herself. "He can't see you through the telephone."

She walked briskly into her bedroom and picked up the receiver, then slumped in relief when she heard Angelica's voice.

"Help!" Diana said faintly.

"What's wrong?"

"My hair. It's . . . it's . . . it's . . . I look like Don King!" she wailed. Covering her face with her hand, she finally gave in to her tears.

"What did you do, Diana?" Angelica asked, cutting through her cousin's sobs.

At Angelica's drill-sergeant tone, Diana took several deep breaths to try to calm herself. "I only wanted . . . to streak it, and . . ."

In between watery hiccups, she somehow managed to explain everything about Adam, her plan, and the forthcoming dinner with his brother.

"Just hang by the phone, kid, until I call you

back," Angelica said, then muttered, "Hell of a way to vamp a man."

"But I don't want—"

The telephone went dead. Diana sat on her bed and thoroughly cursed herself. She shouldn't have attempted such a project on her own, but all the advertisements she'd ever seen claimed it was "easy." The only easy thing had been turning herself into the Bride of Frankenstein. Still calling herself names, she waited impatiently for five minutes, until the telephone rang again.

She snatched up the receiver and said breathlessly, " 'Lo?"

"Get a hat on your head and your buns in your car and meet me at Le Papillon Salon. You've got an appointment there in half an hour. It's just off Union Square on Post. Got it?"

"Yes. I don't know how to thank you—"

"Just go now!"

"Gone!"

Diana slammed the phone down and raced out of her bedroom. She prayed early-afternoon traffic would be light over the Bay Bridge.

It was. Barely. She broke all speed limits, and double-parked her car in front of the elegant shop with less than a minute to spare. Her slender, fashionably dressed cousin was already striding around the front bumper of the car.

"I'll park it," Angelica said, whipping open the driver's door. "Just get in there. Raoul's sarcastic enough when a client's late, let alone shifting around his appointments for an emergency."

Nodding, Diana scrambled out of the car. She jammed the wool watch cap farther down over her ears and ran inside.

A short, wiry man stood inside the doorway. His arms were folded across his chest, his foot tapping impatiently.

She skidded to a halt in front of him. "I'm Diana Windsor, Angelica's cousin—" she began.

"Who cares?" the man said caustically. He was obviously Raoul. "I assume you're hiding whatever garbage you've done to your hair under that ridiculous hat."

Before she could stop him, he yanked the watch cap from her head.

Raoul screamed in horror.

"But, Raoul, you're the only one in the city who has the talent to pull her together," Angelica was saying a short time later.

"The Bay Area," Raoul corrected her haughtily as he peered at Diana's reflection in the mirror.

"The West Coast," Angelica almost purred, and winked at him.

"I want streaks," Diana said stubbornly from her place in the swivel chair. "Sexy-looking streaks."

"You see! She's impossible," Raoul yelled as Angelica moaned.

"I want streaks," Diana repeated as forcefully as possible, ignoring her cousin's strong grip on her shoulder.

"Raoul, surely you can give her streaks, or something," Angelica said in a soothing voice. "After all, you're a master craftsman. The best in the country."

"Welllll . . ."

Diana kept her mouth shut. She knew a rescue when she saw one. By some miracle, her cousin had managed to calm down the temperamental hairstylist and wheedle him into agreeing to repair her hair. She was positive Angelica could pull this off too.

"After I put the red pigments back in the hair shafts," he finally said, "I suppose I could weave the color around some of the already stripped hair. But it will be very difficult. . . ."

"The price is no problem," Angelica said. "A complete make-over comes to—what?—about five hundred dollars?"

Diana gasped and bolted upright in the chair.

"And then there's your bonus. . . ."

"Trudy! Barbara!" the little dictator suddenly shouted around the booth's partition. "Ms. Windsor is getting the works!"

With a resigned sigh, Diana sank back down. For the price she was paying, Adam had better be more than stunned into speechlessness.

He'd better pass right out on the floor.

Eight

"Maybe I should go with you," Angelica said as she straightened the clutter on the bathroom counter.

Diana shook her head. "No. I have to be the one to teach the brothers Roberts a much-needed lesson." Especially one of them, she added to herself. "Well, do you think I look confident and sophisticated?"

Angelica laughed. "I think you'll knock their socks off!"

"I can't thank you enough for your help—"

Angelica waved a hand in dismissal. "I had a blast, but I'd better get going just in case they arrive early." She gave Diana a hug. "Knock 'em dead, kid!"

After Angelica left, Diana sat in her living room and tried to calm her jumping stomach. She admitted she was just a little nervous about Adam's reaction when he saw the new Diana. At least she didn't *look* nervous. She still found it hard to believe the exotically glamorous woman she'd seen in her mirror was actually her!

When Raoul had said "the works," he certainly hadn't been kidding. The sarcastic hairstylist had miraculously brought her hair back to its natural color, while leaving threadlike dramatic blond streaks in it. Then he'd cut her hair to a manageable shoulder length and styled it off her forehead and face, rather like a lion's mane.

But that had been only the beginning. Her face had been analyzed, mud-plastered, and creamed. Her eyebrows had been ruthlessly tamed with tweezers. Her nails had been sculpted an inch longer in a process that still mystified her. Rather than feeling as if the fake ends would pop off at any moment, she wondered how she would ever remove the thick, rosy-pink acrylic without resorting to dynamite. They'd shown her how to use makeup to emphasize her eyes and give herself model-perfect looks. She'd been forced to make up her face five times, until everyone was satisfied that she wouldn't stab herself in the eye with the mascara brush. She'd then carted home a bag of "goodies" that had to have weighed at least ten pounds.

As she attempted to adjust nonexistent glasses on her nose, she chuckled. Her transformation hadn't ended at the beauty salon. Yesterday she'd been fitted with contact lenses. And afterward she must have visited every department store and boutique in San Francisco—with Angelica's help. Her cousin had insisted on taking a day off to accompany her. Diana was immensely grateful; she'd been terrified that she'd pick the wrong outfit and completely ruin the effect she'd wanted. Angelica, though, had had great advice. Angelica also had a streak of daring.

Diana looked down at her dress of shimmering, baby-pleated crepe. That streak of daring must run in the family, she thought.

The violet-blue bodice was sleeveless, with a low scoop neck, and ended in a point just below her belly button. The ankle-length skirt was a deep royal blue. Elliptical cutouts on either side of her waist bared a goodly portion of skin. The dress was daring, deceptively simple, and decidedly elegant. Flat diamond clusters with dripping diamond ropes hung from her ears, and thick white-gold bangles covered her wrists.

She'd never looked so good in her life, she decided. She was positive Adam would never again think of her as a helpless, naïve innocent who could be seduced into a business deal.

Hearing car tires crunch on the gravel driveway, she swallowed back a sudden tidal wave of butterflies and sternly told herself to smile—and just keep smiling. "When it comes to business, always keep 'em guessing, kid," Angelica had said.

She crossed the room, keeping her steps slow and steady and sending heavenward a prayer that she wouldn't teeter off her silver high-heeled sandals and break an ankle. Despite hours of practice, she still wasn't completely at ease wearing them.

The doorbell rang, and she counted to ten before opening the front door.

"Good evening, Adam," she said in a low voice.

Diana fought her laughter as Adam's jaw dropped in astonishment. There was a long silence. Then he blinked once and made a noise as if to speak.

Nothing, though, came out of his mouth. Instead he stared at her, his gaze traveling down her body and up . . . and down and up again. He focused on her face with each pass, as if trying to discern that the Diana he knew was really there.

His reaction was everything she'd hoped for—more, even—and she realized there was a subtle, very feminine power in reducing a man to stunned silence. But she sensed there was also a risk when the *man's* power affected the woman. And Adam had always affected her that way. Instead of congratulating herself on a needed victory, she warned herself to keep all the detachment and distance possible with him.

She turned her attention to Adam's brother, who was also staring in surprise.

"You must be Dan," she said sweetly, and held out her hand to the younger, bespectacled version of Adam. "I've heard a great deal about you."

Taking her hand, Dan smiled. "I was very sorry I missed meeting you at the reception last week."

His hand caused no jolts or nervousness, and she realized that Dan was simply the catalyst for her game. Adam was her true opponent.

"But I'm very happy to finally meet you, Diana," Dan went on, releasing her hand. "May I call you Diana?"

"Of course," she said. "Would you like to come in for a drink before we go to the restaurant?"

"No!" Adam exclaimed, finally coming out of his trance.

She waited a moment for him to say something more. When nothing was forthcoming, she said, "Fine. I'll just get my bag." She turned to the entry table and picked up a tiny white-gold beaded clutch. "I'm ready."

"Don't you need a coat or something?" Adam asked. His eyes narrowed in pointed meaning as he stared at her dress.

"I don't think so. It's very warm out tonight," she said, smiling.

"Get a coat."

Dan suddenly laughed. "You don't want to hide all that beauty under a coat, Adam."

Diana tilted her head. "Why, thank you, Dan. What a nice compliment."

Without waiting for another protest from Adam, she slipped out the door and shut it behind her. She activated her alarm, then turned and faced the men.

"I've been looking forward to this dinner ever since Adam called me this morning to arrange the final details. Shall we go?"

She smiled at Adam when he took her elbow, and, enjoying herself immensely, stepped between the brothers to enter the field of battle.

"Would you pass the lemon . . ."

As Adam looked at Diana to make the simple request, his voice trailed away. Cursing the speechless reaction he'd had every time he'd gazed at the absolutely stunning creature sitting beside him, he cleared his throat and tried again. "Please pass the lemon sauce, Diana."

Smiling, she picked up the silver serving boat and handed it to him. He quickly turned away and began pouring more sauce over his lobster.

How, he wondered, was he supposed to get through dinner without constantly gawking at her? She was more beautiful than ever! It was only

sheer luck that he'd managed not to crash his car
on the drive from her house to L'Etoile restaurant in San Francisco. The more he'd tried to
force himself not to look at her, the more his eyes
had strayed—and stayed—of their own accord.
Somehow, too, he had not given in to the overwhelming urge to carry her away and make every
kind of love imaginable with her. Somehow. It
hadn't been easy to repress the urge to stake a
thorough claim on Diana, especially as she now
continued to draw the gaze of every man in the
restaurant. Even his own brother's eyes had briefly
contained a gleam of primitive male interest,
dammit!

Realizing that he hadn't been paying attention
to his actions and had drowned his lobster in
nearly a pitcherful of lemon sauce, he cursed under his breath again. He set the pitcher on the
snowy-white linen tablecloth. With his fork he
scraped the excess off his food as unobtrusively
as possible. Out of the corner of his eye, he saw
that Dan and Diana, sitting across from each
other, weren't looking his way.

He was grateful that neither of them seemed to
be aware of his sudden loss of social graces. He
hoped their ignorance would continue, since he
was obviously going to make an ass of himself the
entire evening.

Dan took a sip of his champagne. "I've heard
that Genesis Computers recruited you out of Berkeley in your sophomore year, Diana," he said.

"Actually, they yanked me right after I finished
my freshman year," Diana replied. She daintily
patted her mouth with a linen napkin and leaned
back in her Louis Quinze chair.

Adam calmly decided he'd kill if he didn't find those lush lips under his own before the night was gone.

"The companies were pretty desperate then for programmers," she added, and smiled. "What year did they get you?"

"Pinnacle signed me in my freshman year, and I worked for them part-time until I graduated." He sipped some more champagne. "I hope I never see another vacation condo in Hawaii again."

Diana laughed, and Dan joined her. Adam wondered if he'd missed a joke somewhere, because he had no idea why vacation condominiums were so funny. His attention had been diverted by Diana's exposed cleavage. Determined to pay attention to the conversation, he forced his gaze away from the voluptuous sight.

Dan continued. "I always preferred straight stock rather than the use of a condo whenever a company made an offer."

"Yes," Diana replied. "And of course generous royalties."

"Ferraris were a nice inducement too."

"I *prefer* Rolls-Royces."

"A hefty salary never hurt."

"A huge advance is better."

"Management giving free rein on software development was always gratifying."

Diana smiled a tiny smile. "Almost anybody with a rudimentary knowledge of computers could write his own ticket in those days, until the industry shake-out."

Dan nodded. "Although the industry has stabilized, an innovative programmer or engineer is still considered a prized possession by a company."

Adam shook his head, trying to sort through the confusing exchange. He'd grasped that they'd been talking about how they'd entered the computer industry, but there was an underlying current that he didn't understand. It was as if each were trying to top the other with the offers they'd received in the past. Either that, or he was the straight man in a sophisticated repartee with Mr. Spock overtones.

Diana turned to him, her huge violet eyes alight with amusement. It was amazing how much sparkle had been hidden behind her glasses, he thought.

"I'm sorry, Adam. It was rude of Dan and me to reminisce about how fast the computer industry adopted several big-business perks."

"I'm just pleased that you two are getting along," he lied. Diana had more in common with his brother than she had with him, and the thought bothered him immensely. It was disconcerting, too, to admit Daniel wasn't a scrawny kid anymore, but a man. A good-looking man. Adam sternly told himself that Dan might understand Diana's livelihood, but only *he* had a more intimate understanding with her.

To his astonishment, Diana actually winked at his brother. "It surprises me that this one was never bitten by the computer bug, Dan."

"I tried my damnedest to convert him, Diana. But he was always a bear without a good night's sleep, and you know that's when most programmers tend to do their best work."

To Adam's further astonishment, she turned back and winked at *him*. "I suppose it all depends on what you're willing to lose sleep over. Right, Adam?"

"Exactly," he drawled, wanting to establish his right of claim over Diana to everyone at the table.

"Has your company gone public yet, Dan?" she asked.

"Our goal is to take it on the stock exchange next year," he said.

Surprised by Diana's question, Adam interjected, "I didn't know you knew anything about the stock market, Diana."

She grinned. "We Rapunzels have to take a look out of the tower window every so often, Adam."

"Rapunzel?" Dan asked.

She nodded. "Meeting Adam has made me realize just how long I've been locked away from the world—a bit like Rapunzel. Now the world is a new adventure game for me, and I fully intend to test every path possible."

Adam glared at her while wondering just how literally she meant her last remark. As far as he was concerned, they would test every path together. The sooner Diana learned that, the better.

"I'm not sure I understand exactly what you mean. . . ." Dan said slowly.

She waved a hand. "I'm sure Adam will be glad to explain it to you later."

Adam sure would, Adam thought. But first he'd "explain" it to Diana. Obviously she was in need of several more lessons.

Throughout the rest of the dinner, he forced himself to hold up his end of the conversation—and repeatedly reminded himself that he should be pleased Diana and Dan had established a friendly rapport. It was harder, though, to accept the growing realization that the beautiful and provocative Diana would scarcely be in need of a rescue tonight.

Ten minutes after they'd been served coffee and dessert, Adam decided dinner had gone on long enough. "Ready to go?" he asked.

He ignored Diana's glance at her barely touched boysenberry parfait and motioned to the waiter for the check.

"There's no rush, Adam. . . ." Dan began to protest.

"You told me you had an early business appointment tomorrow," Adam said, pointedly raising his eyebrows.

Dan stared at him in bewilderment, then coughed. "Oh . . . ah . . . yes. I'd quite forgotten."

"What a shame the evening has to end so soon," Diana said, smiling at Dan.

A damn shame, Adam thought. It was a damn good thing his brother had taken the hint.

And a damn good thing Diana hadn't.

A short while later, Diana smiled at Dan as he gallantly helped her back into the passenger seat of Adam's Trans Am. They were parked in front of his hotel.

"I've thoroughly enjoyed the evening," Dan said. "Thank you both for keeping me company. I'm glad we finally met, Diana, and I hope we . . . talk again soon."

"I'm sure we will," she murmured demurely.

"I'll give you a call before I leave tomorrow, Adam."

"Good night, Daniel," Adam said dismissingly, and shoved the stick shift into first gear.

Dan had barely closed the passenger door when the Trans Am shot away from the curb with a squeal of tires.

Diana settled back in the bucket seat and closed her eyes. She had taken her contacts out before they left the restaurant, since she was only allowed to wear them for a few hours. She had brought her glasses, but, not wanting to spoil her glamorous image, hadn't put them on. She could see well enough to get around without bumping into anything, anyhow. She definitely wasn't going to need rescuing tonight.

It had been a long evening, but a very successful one. She decided sophistication and confidence were downright easy—once you had the proper tools.

She was quite aware that her little exchange with Dan on past business perks had actually been a subtle bargaining between them about what she might accept for her game. It hadn't mattered what he offered, but it had mattered very much that she pretend to be open to an offer from him. And she'd done it very coolly and smoothly, she decided. Well, maybe she'd gone a little too far with the Rolls-Royce, but what the heck. Angelica would have been proud of her.

Remembering how more than one man had gazed and nodded at her during the evening, Diana smiled. Looking and feeling terrific certainly had its unexpected benefits. Still, none of that attention had affected her the way Adam's looks had. It had been difficult to ignore the melting sensation inside her, and it had been more difficult to maintain her composure whenever his gaze touched her.

Now she became aware of an odd, tense silence in the car, and a thread of uneasiness curled through her veins.

"Your brother is very nice," she said, and opened her eyes to look at Adam.

He spared her a glance before returning his attention to his driving. "I'm glad you liked him."

"Oh, I did. I was sorry his morning appointment cut the evening short. I really enjoyed his company."

"The evening may have ended for Dan, but it hasn't for you and me."

"It hasn't?" she echoed, sitting up straighter in her seat.

"No. I thought we'd have a drink at my place."

She stared at him, her uneasiness growing into dread. "Your place?"

He nodded. "It's much better than a noisy bar, and it also has a terrific view of the bay. We can talk without being disturbed."

She swallowed. "Talk?"

He smiled. "Talk."

Being alone with him was dangerous—especially after a meal. She couldn't . . .

Diana set her jaw. The old Diana would have been nervous and klutzy at the thought of being alone with Adam in his home, but the new Diana had completely controlled the evening. And two men. It was only logical to conclude that the new Diana could also control having a drink in a man's home. And having concluded that, she decided it was also logical that she ought to be able to control the man.

"A drink sounds wonderful," she said, and relaxed back in her seat.

Nine

"You have a beautiful place, Adam," Diana said, gazing around his living room. The furnishings were sparse and neat, and the bright colors of several paintings relieved the near-Spartan effect.

Adam leaned over the back of the sofa, where she was seated, and handed her a glass of Triple Sec. "Thanks. I haven't told you yet how beautiful you look tonight, Diana. I think you were the most beautiful woman in the restaurant, but that dress is . . . rather chilly, isn't it?"

Smoothing a hand over the skirt, she grinned. "No. I'm just fine."

"This is quite a change for you," he said. He walked around the sofa to sit in one of the curved-back armchairs across from her. "May I ask what prompted it?"

She hesitated, her brain scrambling for a careful answer. "I just thought it was time for a change."

"Well, it's a stunning one."

Thanking him for the compliment, she decided she'd been quite right in thinking she could control this part of the evening too. Adam was certainly being a gracious and chivalrous host. It was obvious that he had no idea he was taking his cues from her confident and sophisticated behavior. She really was a very quick learner, she thought. Once she was on the right path. This was turning out to be quite an adventure game.

Still, there was one thing about which she'd been shortsighted, and that was her attraction to Adam. He'd removed his suit jacket after they'd arrived at his apartment, and ever since, she hadn't been able to keep from admiring the lean lines of his body. There was something about a man stripping to informality in front of a woman. . . .

"What other changes do you have in store for me?" he asked.

She smiled down at her tiny liqueur glass. "A few."

"I've always liked surprises. But then, you've always surprised me, Diana. And pleased me."

She felt a tiny quake of warning inside, then dismissed it. "Do you have other relatives besides Dan in Seattle?"

"A few. But let's not talk about them. Let's talk about us."

That tiny quake turned into tremors, and she knew she had to dispel them. "I thought we were. Why did you become an architect?"

He gazed at her with an undecipherable expression, then shrugged. She couldn't tear her gaze away from his mouth as he slowly raised his glass and sipped his drink. Finally he said, "I like the demands of uniting raw materials into a strong structural design. If done properly, the result is visually, physically, and emotionally stimulating."

She swallowed hard. She had a feeling he was talking about something entirely different from architecture. The "ground" was beginning to shake violently.

Suddenly restless, she rose from the couch and strolled as casually as possible across the long room to the big picture window. Taking a quick, reviving sip of the fiery liqueur, she stared out at the night. Without her glasses she could just discern the twinkling lights reflected on the bay's inky surface. "You have a lovely view."

"I think so."

She sensed a surge of male power in his last remark, and, tilting her head slightly, checked to see if he was still in his chair. He was. Thank heavens, she thought. She felt as if she were teetering right on the edge of that damn precipice, and one foolish move on her part would send her plunging downward. Maybe there was still a chance to veer the conversation and atmosphere back into her control. She leaned forward and concentrated on the lighted skyline across the water, hoping to think of some innocuous comment to make.

Suddenly she heard the shocking whisper of footsteps directly behind her. Move, she told herself. Keep a distance between them. Say something, anything, that might possibly halt his progress. Be sophisticated and confident.

Instead, every fiber of her being froze as Adam neared her and stopped directly behind her.

"Princesses should know better than to test knights' honor," he murmured, lifting the hair from the nape of her neck. "Tonight has made it all too clear that you are in dire need of a rescuing, Diana."

She felt the floor shift wildly under her feet when his mouth touched the sensitive flesh he'd exposed. For long minutes his lips and tongue charted a sensual journey over every inch of exposed skin on her neck and shoulders. Delicate chills coursed down her spine, until she was shaking with the effort to keep from sagging back against him.

Blindly she reached out with her free hand and grasped the windowsill in a desperate attempt to hold herself upright. As she gasped for breath, she dimly wondered what had happened to all the air in the room. A moan escaped her as Adam's hands glided across the bared skin at her waist. Her liqueur glass was taken from her and set on the sill, and then he pressed himself into her back.

Without thought, she melted against him. His strong fingers tightened across her belly, lifting her against his growing arousal.

"I want you," he whispered, and traced the fragile shell of her ear with kisses. "I need to know you're mine. Only mine."

Diana felt as if she were caught in a raging fire and swirling tornado all at once. Her body burned. Her flesh quivered. She was totally out of control at the evidence of his raw need. But this shouldn't have been happening. She should stop him. He'd given her the power to stop him with just one word.

Still, in spite of knowing the price she would pay later, she was incapable of halting him. In spite of knowing it was all wrong, she realized nothing had ever felt so right.

She turned her head, instinctively seeking and finding his mouth with her own. Her tongue intertwined with his with an urgency that belied all gentleness. His arms tightened around her in a hard embrace, and she reached up and threaded her fingers through his hair to pull his mouth impossibly closer.

His mind reeling at her boldness, Adam slipped his hands up her silken flesh, beneath her dress, until he found the thrusting mounds of her breasts. He lightly rubbed his palms across the hard nipples. His fingers danced over them, loving the way they grew even harder at his touch. With his lips he caressed the throbbing pulse on the side of her slender neck.

All his repressed rights as protector had finally demanded satisfaction when he'd heard her coyly flirt with his brother outside the hotel. His own brother! He'd instantly realized he'd been too chivalrous with her. It had been his own fault that he hadn't made certain the princess understood what it meant when she granted a knight claim over her. Tonight he would clarify that little oversight to the satisfaction of them both.

He lifted his head and turned her in his arms, his fingers finding the hidden zipper of her dress.

"You're mine, princess," he repeated harshly. "Only mine."

Her arms tightened around him in answer. He tried to control the trembling in his hands as he slowly lowered the zipper, then he pushed the dress off her shoulders and down her arms. It dropped to a shimmering pool at her ankles. His breath whistled out of his lungs at the feel of her skin under his hands. He traced the incredible satin of her spine and sank his fingers into the soft roundness of her derriere. Only her half-slip and panties prevented him from exploring further.

He covered her mouth in a deep kiss. He wanted to kiss her forever. After tonight he *would* kiss her forever.

Her hands tugged at his shoulders in supplication, making him forget all thoughts of a bed. Barely breaking the kiss, he pulled her to the floor with him. She lay in his arms with a trust and acquiescence that made all the blood in his body pound deafeningly. Her coral-tipped breasts teased him in invitation. As he lowered his head to kiss them, he knew he would never break that trust.

"I love you," he whispered, and nuzzled at a velvety nipple.

At his words, Diana felt a dark, tender mist close over her. This was why it was so right, she thought. This was love.

Shamelessly she guided his tormenting lips over her aching breasts. With swirling tongue and soft bites he drove her to the edge of sanity. Her body twisted uncontrollably under the sensual onslaught, and she was barely aware of his stripping away the last of her clothes. He trailed kisses down her stomach, around her navel, and downward still, over the tender flesh of her thighs.

Slowly he began retracing his path upward, and of their own accord her fingers reached for the buttons on his shirt. She tried to undo them, but her hands fumbled, and he gently brushed them aside. His mouth still working its magic on her flesh, he scrambled out of his own clothes.

With a sureness born of passion, Diana smoothed her hands across the hard planes of his muscled back. She delighted in the dense swath of curling hair on his chest and the well-defined torso underneath. Everywhere she touched was virile male, made for her.

His knowing hand aroused her until she was mindlessly writhing against it. Then his body covered hers. His hips fit into the cradle of her soft thighs. She felt no fear, only need and want, as he carefully probed the silken moistness of her femininity. With one long, sure stroke, he thrust inside, and she cried out at the wonder of it.

"I hurt you," he whispered, burying his lips in the base of her throat. "I'm sorry."

"There's no pain," she reassured him as her body quickly adjusted to his invasion. She began to throb in anticipation. "I . . . Adam, please ... . I love you . . . don't stop."

He kissed her dampened skin and murmured, "I can't stop. I love you. Wrap your legs around my waist."

She did as he instructed, and he raised himself on his elbows. With slow movements he withdrew, then filled her, again and again.

Instinctively she moved her hips once to meet his, then twice, until she was following the ancient rhythm with him. She felt an incredible tension building inside her and clutched at his shoulders as protection against the sensual rampage. As if sensing the tumult within her, he quickened the pace, thrusting faster and harder.

Her very being seemed to shatter suddenly into bright shards of light that mingled with Adam's throbbing release. Then a satin darkness enfolded them.

Diana gradually became aware of her surroundings when she heard Adam say, "I'm sorry."

"Why?" she asked lazily. His body was pressing hers into the plush carpeting, yet she wasn't the least uncomfortable.

"It was your first time. You deserved a bed with silk sheets and—"

"Do you have silk sheets?" she asked, languidly stroking his shoulders.

"Well, no."

"Then my first time wouldn't have been in a bed with silk sheets." She turned her head to look at him. "How do silk sheets make it better?"

He blinked, confusion replacing the slight regret in his brown eyes. "It would have made it more special. . . ."

She smiled. "Nothing could have made it more special, Adam. Nothing."

His arms tightened around her, and he kissed the pulse point just under her ear. "I love you, Diana."

She knew the words came from his heart, and she closed her eyes in pain. She'd been foolish, but now she realized her foolishness had been in suspecting Adam of having any part in getting her to sell her game to his brother. No man who exhibited any kind of honor would do such a thing. And Adam was a very honorable man. An innocent man. Tonight had made her see the final and total truth. Dan had used Adam, and, to her shame, so had she.

She resisted the overwhelming urge to beg his forgiveness, knowing that it might cause a rift with his brother. And any confession would probably kill his feelings for her. She'd be crazy to jeopardize that. It would be best if she said nothing, and instead gave him her trust and love in every way possible. Then, she hoped, she could remove the guilt of her own duplicity.

"I suppose," she began in a trembling voice as her emotions played havoc inside her, "that we could get some silk sheets and see if they're all you think they're cracked up to be. . . ."

He smiled down at her.

"Personally," she continued, "I don't think anything would make it better, but if the teacher wants silk sheets—"

"Forget I ever mentioned silk sheets," he ordered affectionately.

"I saw an advertisement once for satin sheets," she said. "Now they sound a little kinky. Maybe you'd like them bet—"

Her words were abruptly cut off by his hard, fierce kiss. Running her hands down his sides and over his buttocks, she shuddered at his renewed arousal. And her own.

"I love you, Adam," she murmured when he lifted his head. "Love me again."

And he did.

"Plain old cotton sheets," Diana said sadly as she snuggled against Adam's side in his bed later. "I hope you're not too disappointed."

She yelped when he pinched her bare bottom.

"Keep it up," he said, "and you'll be wishing you never heard of the damn things."

She wiggled around until she was half-lying across his chest. Propping her chin on her folded arms, she said chidingly, "You're no fun. Okay, silk and satin sheets are out. Now, I've heard some things about mirrors—"

"Diana! Go to sleep."

She sighed and spread her hand across his dark chest hair. For long moments she just twirled the short, silky strands around her fingers, occasionally placing a kiss on his warm skin.

"You're not sleeping," Adam finally said, his arm tightening around her waist.

"Mmmm." Laying her head on his chest, she smiled as she trailed her hand down his biceps. "I was just thinking that I met you only ten days ago."

"I think how we feel is more important than how much time it takes for us to feel that way," he said, stroking her hair.

"I just didn't want to rush you, or anything." She sighed dramatically. "Still, it *might* be too soon for the mirrors. . . ."

He gently tugged her hair in reprimand. "You'll be sorry in the morning if you keep talking like that."

"And how is that?"

"Making love is like exercise. If you don't take it easy in the beginning, you'll feel it the next day."

"No pain, no gain," she quipped, rubbing her breasts against his chest.

"I'm trying to be a gentleman. . . ."

"I suppose I should stop teasing you. After all, you are older and—"

In one swift movement, Adam reversed their positions.

"I'm such a wicked woman," she murmured just before his mouth covered hers.

"Diana. Wake up, honey."

As Adam's voice penetrated her layers of sleep, Diana smiled. She snuggled back against the delicious warmth of his body and sighed. The morning had brought no regrets, no second thoughts. This was where she belonged.

Adam kissed her shoulder, her hair. . . .

"Five more minutes, Mom," she mumbled.

"Diana!"

She pulled the pillow across her face to smother her laughter. He yanked it out of her hands and glared down at her.

"I'm sorry," she gasped out between giggles. "But I just couldn't resist."

"If you ever do it again, I swear I'll tell you that you snore."

"I do not!"

He smiled evilly.

"Do I?" she asked in a tiny voice, mortified at the thought of having done such a thing in his presence.

"You'll never know." He kissed her nose, then brushed something off her cheek. "That's strange. There are tiny flecks of soot on your cheeks."

"Soot?" she repeated. Then her eyes widened. Her mascara must have smeared during the night. Embarrassed, she covered her face with her hands and muttered, "Where's the bathroom?"

"The bathroom door is next to the bureau. What's the matter?"

"Nothing. I just want to . . . ah . . . use the facilities." She slid a bare leg off the bed, then realized the rest of her was just as bare. Her blood heated her face. "Could you get me a robe or something, Adam?"

"In a minute." His fingers pried at hers, but she resisted his pulling them away. "Your face is red, Diana, so I know you're upset about something. Please don't shut me out. Not now."

She dropped her hands and wailed, "The damn mascara ran, and I probably look like a raccoon! That's why I'm upset."

"You do *not* look like a raccoon," he said, taking her in his arms. "You look like a woman well loved, and I'm proud to be the man who's made you look that way."

"You're lying through your teeth, Adam Roberts," she said, deciding repairs at this point were useless anyway. The damage was already done, and she might as well accept it. "But I love you for it. Now will you let me up so I can use the bathroom? My mouth tastes like a cow pasture."

He groaned and rolled onto his back. "I'm going to have to give you a lesson on how *not* to kill the mood."

Ten

Adam was smiling as he retrieved Diana's clothing from his living room. It had been an incredible night, and he hated the thought of its ending.

As he walked back into the bedroom, he admitted that he hadn't allowed Diana to decide consciously if she wanted to make love. Instead he'd seduced her into it, quite ruthlessly. But he'd been desperate. Witnessing her metamorphosis had driven him nearly insane. She was his. He knew it, and she had seemed to know it too. He'd understood that she'd only been testing her feminine appeal to other men, but he'd been afraid that she would like the experiment and decide to "expand her horizons." He had no regrets about forcing their relationship onto a more intimate level, and he was damn grateful that Diana didn't either. Although he firmly believed that time would make no difference to their feelings, he realized he couldn't rush her into anything else. She had to be very sure of both herself and him before that.

He knocked on the bathroom door. "Diana?"

The door opened a few inches and a long-nailed hand reached out for the clothes. He grinned as he handed them over. The door closed.

"I still haven't figured out how you grew those nails in two days," he said through the door.

"I haven't figured out how I'm going to type on a keyboard without the darn things hooking in between the keys," she called back. "You'll probably have to rescue me again."

He chuckled.

"I think torture chambers are masquerading as beauty salons nowadays," she continued. "I've been sculpted, creamed, masked, waxed, plucked, cut, washed, and dried by a real nasty named Raoul and his two very nice assistants." She sighed loudly. "It was wonderful."

At her obvious ecstasy, Adam burst into laughter. Diana was very much a woman, to endure such horrors and actually think of it as pampering. Still, he had to admit the results were devastating to a man. Lord, but she had looked gorgeous. And it was very evident she had done it for him.

There was no sense telling her he'd always found her sexy as hell, he thought. After all she'd gone through, he doubted she'd appreciate the compliment.

"If I didn't have this damned hotel annex to work on, I wouldn't be taking you home," he said, hoping she understood why he couldn't spend the day with her. Hell, he thought. Of all times.

"Don't worry about it, Adam. I'll see you tonight." There was a pause. "*Will* I see you tonight?"

"Diana, I'll torture myself today because of my obligations. But I will not torture myself beyond that. We'll have the whole weekend together. And more."

"Good."

He relaxed against the door. They'd probably spend the weekend at her house, and he couldn't think of a more perfect place to be. Hidden away in the Berkeley Hills, her computer on guard against intruders, it would be a refuge where they could make love and talk.

Realizing he'd end up spending the weekend trapped at the office if he didn't get dressed and take Diana home, he straightened and banged on the door.

"Get a move on, Diana. A knight is only chivalrous for so long when it comes to the bathroom!"

"I feel like a . . . wanton, coming home in my gown at nine in the morning," Diana said as Adam's Trans Am turned onto the long, shaded drive of her property.

"By rights you should be back in my bed being a naked wanton," Adam said. "Tonight, though, you can start being a wanton for the weekend."

She grinned. "With mirrors?"

"You'd better be careful," he warned her. "You might just get what you ask for."

It was amazing how natural she felt with Adam now, Diana thought. While her mind had been sidetracked by doubts and suspicions, her heart had been heading in the right direction all along. Still, she wouldn't have realized how she felt about him—or how he felt about her—if she hadn't acted on those doubts and suspicions. She idly wondered how long she still would have foundered if she hadn't instigated the showdown with Adam and his brother. At this point she wasn't sure whether she should thank Dan or murder him for the trouble he'd caused. She would have to talk to him soon, though, making it very clear that her relationship with Adam would in no way affect to whom her games were finally sold.

That thought brought on a more frightening one. What if Adam got upset if she didn't sell her games to his brother? Unfortunately, Dan's low offer already made that a real possibility.

"I'll be back around five-thirty," Adam said, breaking into her thoughts.

Realizing the car was nearing her front door, she nodded, and said, "I'll cook dinner."

"I'll bring dinner," he corrected her as he parked next to the deck. "I don't want you wasting energy cooking anything but me."

She shook her head. "I always knew you weren't a knight in shining armor."

"Found out at last."

As he took her in his arms, she sternly told herself not to worry about imagined problems until they actually did happen. Surely they could be worked out. Surely.

Adam suddenly turned away before he'd kissed her, and she realized that something at the house had caught his attention. She followed his gaze, and to her surprise she saw her cousin Angelica striding out the front door. A flush rose instantly to her cheeks.

"Who's that?" Adam asked, releasing her and straightening.

"My cousin." She opened the passenger door. "I wonder what she's doing here."

Angelica leaned over the deck railing and demanded, "Where the hell have you been, Diana?"

Diana stepped out of the car and shut the door behind her. She wanted to curse heartily at her cousin's interruption. And honestly, she thought as she heard Adam getting out of the car, Angelica wasn't an idiot. Adam's presence ought to be self-explanatory.

Still she stammered. "Well . . . ah . . ."

"You'd better get in here," Angelica broke in. "I can't figure out what's missing, and—"

"Missing!" Diana yelped.

"You had a break-in last night."

Diana raced up the steps. "That's impossible! Charlie was on duty. . . ."

Not wasting any more words, she ran into the house and headed straight for the workroom. Nothing could circumvent her computer, she thought wildly. Charlie couldn't be enticed with a piece of drugged meat, as a dog might. Charlie couldn't be bribed. He was even battery-backed in case of a power failure. She checked him every day to make sure he was working properly. . . .

"Nooooo!" she screamed, skidding to a halt on the threshold of the workroom.

It was a shambles. Chairs were overturned, papers, books, and disks were strewn everywhere, and the bookcases were lying on the floor like rusted ships left to rot in the shallows.

Curiously enough, the computers themselves seemed untouched. Then she spotted Charlie, and cried out a second time.

She ran over and knelt on the floor next to the

smashed console and broken circuit boards that had once been her favorite computer. Tears coursed down her cheeks as she touched the wreckage in disbelief.

"Diana!" Angelica exclaimed as she came into the room.

Diana barely heard her, or Adam's barnyard curse.

"They killed Charlie," she whispered.

Angelica knelt beside her and put an arm around her. "I know, kid. I'm sorry."

"He was old and outdated . . . but he was my first computer. I learned how to program on him . . . he had such a lovely screen editor. And now he's . . . dead!"

Diana burst into tears. She knew it was irrational to cry over an inanimate object, but in an odd way Charlie had always seemed alive to her. He talked back, scolded her with beeps on occasion, and was contrary whenever she wanted him to do something difficult. He had had a unique quirkiness that had always made her think of him as an individual. And now he was gone.

Suddenly she was in Adam's soothing arms. She pressed her face against his chest and sobbed.

"Go ahead and cry it out, sweetheart," he said as he patted her back.

She cried for a long time, until all she had left inside her were watery hiccups. Gulping them back, she tried to calm herself.

"This place is a fortress," Adam said. "How could burglars have gotten past the alarm system?"

"The police aren't sure," Angelica replied. "They told me they always thought nobody could break in here. As far as they can tell, though, the people

who did it certainly knew what they were doing.
The police think the phone line was cut first, so
the computer's automatic police call wouldn't go
through, and then the sliding glass doors were
smashed. The only way to stop the outside alarm
was to destroy the computer. Someone who was
passing by happened to hear the alarm before it
was cut off, and called the police. When the police
couldn't get Diana, they called me."

Nobody spoke for a moment. Then Adam asked,
"Sweetheart, do you think you're ready to start
sorting through the mess?"

Sniffling, Diana looked up into his concerned
face and nodded. She gazed around the room again
and said, "At least my equipment looks okay. Except . . . Charlie."

"That's odd," Adam said. "Although it's possible
it was just vandals. The damage looks as if it were
done more to destroy than for the sake of burglary."

"Vandals are usually kids," Angelica said. "I can't
imagine kids going this far and passing up a free
computer, can you? Besides, no other room in
the house has been touched."

Adam frowned. "Maybe the police scared them
away before they could take very much."

Diana gasped at his words. She hadn't even
considered what might have been stolen! If the
thieves had gotten her Sir Morbid game, and if
they realized that it was the first adventure game
to utilize voice capabilities, they could also realize how much it would be worth to a software
company. . . .

She pulled herself out of his arms and ran over
to the far wall, where the coin-operated games
stood. Sitting on her heels, she carefully exam-

ined the side panel of one of the games, then pressed her fingers along a thread-sized crack. The hidden panel flap swung outward, and she slumped in relief at the sight of a small square lead box. She lifted it out and opened it. Her disks were safely tucked inside—none missing. There were other copies hidden in different parts of the house, but since the intruders had only disturbed this room, the additional disks were probably still safe.

"Is it there?" Angelica asked.

"Sir Morbid is still with us." With a smile, Diana returned the box to its hiding place, then rose to her feet.

Angelica shook her head. "You've got to be kidding! That's so open and easy!"

"No, it's not," Diana said. "Anyway, these aren't the only copies I have of the Sir Morbid game, but they're the only ones in this room. Disks are easy to hide as long as you're careful about magnetic fields from TVs—"

"What about these others?" Adam asked as he bent down and picked up several disks from the floor.

"I'm not as concerned about those as I am about my games in progress," she answered, stepping around the mess on the floor as she walked over to him. "I don't bother to hide software that's already been published and copyrighted, as these are. I wouldn't lose a livelihood if they were stolen. But I'll have to go through them to be sure none are missing. From the number on the floor, though, I'd have to say that most of them are here. And that's odd." She took one out of his hand and held it up. "This one alone retails for several hundred dollars."

"You're kidding!" Adam exclaimed, staring in disbelief at the little black cardboard squares he still held.

"Nope. It's not the value of the materials, but the amount of time that goes into creating a program, that makes it so costly. A complicated business program can take a team of programmers years to bring to a salable state. The burglars must have been very dumb not to know that these would still be worth a pretty penny to an unscrupulous computer enthusiast."

"Or to the copy crackers," Angelica added. She began to collect some of the scattered disks.

"What are copy crackers?" Adam asked, his brows drawn together in puzzlement.

"People who crack a program's protection scheme and make copies to distribute," Diana said. She took the rest of the disks from him and made a mental note of the titles before setting them on a table.

"You've heard of bootleg records and tapes?" Angelica asked.

He nodded.

"Well, the software business has the same problem, in spite of the copy-protection schemes built into the programs. One out of every ten copies of Diana's already published games is an illegal one. I figure just on 'Space Pirates' alone she's lost about half a million in royalties from illegal copies. That, mind you, is at less than two dollars in royalties per copy."

"Can't something be done?" Adam asked.

"Those caught are prosecuted to the hilt, but

it's tough to catch them. I'm eternally grateful the burglars didn't get any games Diana's working on now. You can't copyright an idea, and until a program is submitted to a company it's only considered an idea by the law. Those who did this could have sold it on their own, and Diana would have received nothing."

"Then it's a damn good thing the bastards didn't know what they were doing," Adam said in a cold voice. "Because I would have killed them."

"My hero," Diana murmured affectionately, and kissed his cheek.

He drew her into his embrace. "If you had been here alone last night . . ."

She wrapped her arms about his waist in answer. She was feeling better, although she still shuddered at the thought of how easily her home had been invaded. Her workroom was a disaster, but obviously the intruders had been scared away before they could take anything of real value. They'd probably done a quick trashing for revenge.

A dreadful thought occurred to her, and she whispered, "What if they come back?"

Adam's arms tightened. "I'll be here."

She nodded, feeling safe and protected. She would always be safe with him. Then she remembered that he needed to be at his job that morning.

Reluctantly she stepped away from him. "You have to get to work, Adam, and I have to clean up this mess and talk to the police."

"First I'll help you clean up," he said, "then I'll go to the office. But I'd better call John."

"No phone," Angelica said. "The line was cut, remember."

"Damn!"

"Good," Diana said sternly, her hands on her hips. "Now you have to go to work. . . ."

Half an hour later Diana sighed with resignation as she watched Adam right the bookcases. In truth, she was secretly glad to have lost the argument. Adam had taken charge and sent Angelica down to a neighbor's to phone his partner, then to call the phone company to fix the outside line and to get someone to replace the broken glass on the sliding door. Diana's job was to find out what was missing. She'd already checked her other "safes," and none of them had been disturbed either. Then she'd changed into jeans and a T-shirt before tackling the workroom.

She smiled, remembering the gleam of appreciation in Adam's eyes when she'd reentered the room. It was the same look he'd given her the night before.

Promising herself she could daydream later, Diana concentrated on sorting through the mess. She created manageable piles of papers, books, and disks by type and subject. After returning from her errand, Angelica began to help. Adam put the books and manuals back on the shelves.

As Diana worked her way from one end of the room to the other, her initial relief at having only possible minor losses was slowly replaced by a growing apprehension. Finally, she set the last piece of notepaper on its proper pile, and claws of fear raked her spine.

"My source codes are gone," she whispered, sending a last desperate glance around the room.

"Your what?" Angelica asked in puzzlement.

Focusing on her cousin, Diana swallowed. "The

hard copy for the game. I printed out the program the other day, because I had a slight problem with the game's graphics. It's easier to find the mistakes on paper than it is on a monitor screen. Now the papers are gone."

Angelica's shoulders slumped in defeat. "The whole program? On paper?"

Diana nodded.

"Why didn't you lock that away too?"

Diana closed her eyes. "The papers are too big to fit in my cubbyholes, so I mixed them up with others that just had a lot of junk on them. It was the hide-in-plain-sight theory."

Angelica cursed loudly.

"What's the problem?" Adam asked as he picked up another load of books.

Her insides numb, Diana explained about her source codes. He dropped the books and knelt beside her, hugging her in silent comfort.

"So they got what they were looking for after all," Angelica said in a cold voice. "Everything seemed so odd, didn't it? I couldn't understand how people who knew exactly how to get around the computer alarm system didn't seem to know what computer stuff to take once they were inside. And they took the time to trash the place, but not the time to search. They probably went through the disks on the tables first, and when they didn't find the game, they went for the computer print-outs. They were more lucky there."

"Not luck," Diana said, beginning to tremble with fury and helplessness. "Anyone who knows about programming would realize that I'd probably have a print-out somewhere."

"But who knows about how your alarm works?" Adam asked.

"That wouldn't matter," she said. She stood up, and he did as well. "It would be dead easy for anyone who knows about alarm systems. They're always vulnerable at the phone line because that can be cut without triggering the alarm itself. Then the police can't be called. You saw how easily the rest of the system was . . . disarmed."

"The game would be worth hundreds of thousands to a software company," Angelica said slowly, turning her eyes to Adam. "If not millions. Someone could have become tired of making offers for the game. Offers that weren't being accepted. Or that were being stalled."

Pain tore through Diana's body.

"Someone," Angelica went on, "who knew exactly what to look for. Someone who knew Diana probably wouldn't be home until very late last night, or possibly not at all. Someone who decided to take advantage of that. And maybe that someone had a partner who was romancing Diana all along just to keep her busy and off-guard."

Diana cried out in agony at her cousin's destructive reasoning. She didn't believe it. Refused to believe it. But, heaven help her, it sounded so horribly logical.

"Are you implying that I had something to do with this?" Adam demanded.

Eleven

Adam forced himself to rein in his temper at Angelica's incredible line of reasoning. He couldn't imagine anyone even thinking that he'd had any part in the break-in. And who the hell was supposed to be his "partner"? The whole idea was laughable—completely and totally laughable.

Then he realized Diana wasn't laughing.

"Starlight Software has made several offers in the past for Diana's latest game," Angelica said in a very soft voice, drawing his shocked attention back to her. "They were all turned down as too low. We didn't hear from Starlight again. Then Diana met you. Suddenly, this past Monday, we received yet another offer, from the president of Starlight. I believe that's your brother. Tuesday he made an appointment to see me on Thursday to discuss the offer further, then abruptly canceled it later that same day. Thursday night—last night—Diana went out to dinner with the two of you. It's obvious that she spent the night with you. You have been in this house before, in this room, and you knew what kind of alarm system there was. I can only wonder about the sudden renewed interest of Starlight. And having dealt before with Starlight's high-pressure tactics, I also wonder just how far such people would go to 'acquire' a game." She turned to her cousin. "I'm sorry, Diana. But the circumstantial evidence is overwhelmingly against him and his brother."

As Angelica spoke, Adam watched Diana's face. There was no trust, no belief in him in her violet eyes; only a knowing sadness and pain. Her cousin's reasoning was outlandish, and yet Diana believed it.

"My brother *might* have bid for Diana's games," he said between clenched teeth. "But you're crazy to think he or I had anything to do with the missing source codes."

"Adam, Dan did bid on the game," Diana whispered, her eyes not meeting his.

Her words staggered him like a driving punch to the solar plexus. They were a confirmation of everything her cousin had said. Diana really believed he was capable of being involved in some stupid scheme to get her game.

He stood up, unconsciously curling his hands into fists. But he didn't hit anything, in spite of the overwhelming urge to do so.

Instead he turned around and walked out the door.

Diana cried. She cried until she was emotionally drained and almost physically sick from weeping so much. Angelica had given her a full box of tissues and left her alone with her grief while she quietly dealt with the telephone-repair man and the glazier from the hardware store.

"A few things are back to normal, kid," Angelica said as she rehung the curtains over the repaired door.

Wiping her eyes with the last of the tissues, Diana said, "You were wrong about Adam."

"No, I wasn't. But I do understand what you're feeling, Diana. It's obvious that you're in love with the man—"

"That's right," Diana broke in, getting to her feet. She turned to face her cousin. "And I shouldn't have doubted him for a moment. But I did. For one tiny instant, I did believe he could have done it."

Shaking her head, Angelica stepped down from the chair she'd been standing on and walked over to Diana.

"There's a fact of life you ought to learn now, Diana," she said, putting her hands on her cousin's shoulders. "Women always fall in love with their first man. And women fall in love with the wrong kind of man. Face the truth, Diana. Adam used you, and in the worst way. It happens to a lot of women. The only good thing about it is that you'll be wiser in love next time. I was."

"Maybe Dan had something to do with stealing my source codes," Diana said in a strong voice. "But not Adam. Adam has honor. He has so much honor that he didn't try to defend himself. He just walked out the door. I admit I was shocked by the direction you were heading in, but I should have straightened you out on that point—"

"You're not objective about this, and right now

that's understandable. But think about who else might have wanted your game so badly that they would have stolen your source codes."

"Anybody!" Diana snapped impatiently. "What you're pointing the finger at Starlight for, any number of other companies might have done. I realize it looks like Dan did it, and he very well could have. I don't know him. But I know Adam."

"What you know is a skillfully created illusion," Angelica retorted, her hands on her hips. "Adam Roberts may be a lot of things, but he didn't strike me as someone who could be played for a chump by his own brother!"

The ringing of the doorbell interrupted Angelica. "I'll get the damn door," she said. "Meantime, you try finding a plausible substitute for the brothers. I doubt if you can."

"And you try finding a little hard evidence against Adam," Diana said, glaring at her cousin. "I doubt if you can either."

Angelica swung around and marched out of the workroom.

Diana rubbed her temples in exasperation. Damn Angelica and her circumstantial evidence, she thought. And she should have kept her mouth shut about Adam when she'd ruined her hair. Then Angelica wouldn't have drawn her terrible conclusions.

With a groan Diana realized she shouldn't be trying to convince Angelica of Adam's innocence. She should be trying to convince Adam of her trust in him. She wished she could replay that terrible moment when her cousin had accused Adam. She should immediately have shouted her faith in him.

"Where's Diana?"

She jumped at the sound of the familiar voice coming from the front of the house. Adam! Feeling as if she'd just been granted a miracle, she ran through the hallway into the living room . . . and stopped dead when he turned toward her. His expression was hard and his eyes were cold.

Seeing Dan with him, she guessed their visit wouldn't be pleasant. She swallowed back a lump of butterflies.

"Now, will you tell me what the hell this is all about, Adam?" Dan asked angrily. "And it had better be damn good to make me miss my appointment."

"This way," Adam snapped, and dragged his brother by the arm toward the workroom.

"Diana, do you know what's turned him into a Grue?" Dan asked in a genuinely frustrated tone as they passed her.

She never had an opportunity to answer Dan, for Adam practically yanked him the rest of the way into the workroom. She and Angelica trotted after them.

"What's a Grue?" Angelica asked.

In spite of her growing fear and depression, Diana chuckled. "A real nasty from the Zork games. You wouldn't want to be one."

Once in the workroom, Adam stopped his mad rush. Dan looked around the almost-straightened room.

"Much as I can appreciate the scope of Diana's working environment," he said, "I could have waited until another time to see it, Adam. Now, what the hell is going on?" he shouted.

"This place was broken into last night," Adam

said, folding his arms across his chest. "And Diana's source codes for her new game were stolen." He paused. "And you and I are accused of doing it."

Dan's mouth dropped open, and he stared wide-eyed at Adam. Finally he closed his mouth and seemed to pull himself together to speak. Then his mouth dropped open again. His astonishment and bewilderment were obvious and genuine.

"I rest my case, counselor," Adam said to Angelica.

Angelica just raised an eyebrow.

Dan managed at last to recover from his shock, and asked, "But why would anyone think that?"

Adam tilted his head toward Angelica, and Diana braced herself for the coming confrontation. She only hoped her cousin would keep her out of it.

Angelica smiled, and replied smoothly, "Because you have not been satisfied with my client's refusals of your low bids for her games. Yet you have not offered an equitable price. When your brother made personal contact with my client, we became suspicious of his motives."

Diana died a little at Angelica's words. Before she could protest, her cousin continued in her blunt, professional voice.

"Our suspicions were rewarded when you made yet another offer and were insistent that my client be told of it. I advised my client that your tone was one of confidence that your offer would be accepted this time—in spite of the same offer being turned down months before. My client then stalled about giving an answer, deciding to investigate a possible connection—"

"Angelica," Diana interrupted.

"—between her personal relationship with Mr. Roberts and the acquisition of her game."

"Angelica!"

"She concluded a connection was quite valid when a dinner invitation from the two of you was forthcoming—"

"*Angelica!*"

"—and was determined to foil any attempts to coerce her into parting with her game on your terms."

"ANGELICA!"

"You must have been quite aware that my client would be away from her home after the dinner was over. You made an appointment with me, then canceled it. Then my client's source codes were stolen. It was only a logical step to further conclude that you and Mr. Roberts had a possible connection with the theft. I came to that conclusion and expressed it to my client and to Mr. Roberts."

To Diana's unhappy relief, Angelica finally shut up. In the tense silence that followed, Diana couldn't look at Adam. She didn't want to see the anger and accusation that must be in his eyes. In stating her points, Angelica had managed to nail the coffin lid shut on a reconciliation with him. He'd never understand now, she thought despairingly. She knew she wouldn't if the circumstances were reversed.

"Ms. Windsor," Dan finally said.

Diana glanced up, then realized his gaze was directed at Angelica. His expression was as cold and hard as Adam's, and he was visibly restraining his anger. "I do not refute that my company made several offers for your client's games," he said. "That is a fact. Unhappily, when I was informed of her continued refusals, I discovered that my acquisitions manager had attempted techniques of persuasion that I abhor. He was fired. At the time, I felt it was best to withdraw from further negotiations, as your client was most likely offended. I attended the Omega reception with the intention of introducing myself to your client and possibly reopening negotiations. My brother, though, met your client first and agreed to help with the completion of her game. When I learned from my brother that she was still agreeable to him even after the article in *CompuWorld*—"

"What article?" Adam asked.

Dan turned to him. "After the reception where you met Diana, Jim Griegson printed a blurb that you would be helping me get Diana for Starlight. It was one of Jim's nasty speculations—totally untrue—and that's probably where this whole mess started."

Hot anger blazed out of Adam's eyes as he swung his gaze toward Diana. She turned her head away in shame. She knew he was wondering why she hadn't just asked him about it. Even if she had, she doubted that she would have believed him at the time.

"I only hoped that your client might look favorably upon Starlight again," Dan said, his tone formal once more as he continued speaking to Angelica. "I made another offer. A *reasonable* offer. You did not decline this time, so I made an appointment with you to discuss further terms. Then I discovered my brother had a personal interest in your client. I canceled the appointment and planned to withdraw my offer after explaining to my brother my inadvertent interference in his personal life. That opportunity has not arisen until, unfortunately, now. My brother had no knowledge of any of this, and I hope he will one day forgive me. I am sorry, too, for any distress my offers have caused your client. I state for the record that I did not, either personally or through agents, steal your client's source codes. That you have concluded thus is irresponsible and ludicrous—"

"Irresponsible!" Angelica yelled, losing all her lawyer's poise.

"—and stupid!" Dan shouted back, waving his arms wildly. "I ought to take you to court for slander!"

"You give back Diana's source codes now and sign a form stating you will never publish any of her games, and maybe we won't have you thrown in jail for grand larceny! Maybe!"

As the two of them began an all-out shouting match, Diana quietly stepped over to Adam and tugged at his white shirt sleeve. If she could get him to talk to her, she might be able to make him understand. . . .

"Adam. I can explain—"

"Don't bother," he said coldly. "You used me, Diana. I can never forgive that."

"Adam, please listen," she begged, tears clogging her throat. "It wasn't quite—"

"Don't. Because I won't believe you, just as you didn't believe me."

He walked away from her to stand at the door to the hall and wait for his brother.

Diana took a deep breath to hold back her tears. What could she—

The telephone rang suddenly. Startled, she whirled around and stared at it. Everybody did. A second shrill ring blasted in the now-quiet room.

Diana walked over to the phone, picked up the receiver, and said, "Hello?"

"I have your source codes," a muffled voice said.

Her heart leaping at the words, Diana grasped the receiver tightly. "Thank heavens!" Now Angelica would have to believe the thief wasn't Adam, she thought.

The voice continued. "You have one chance to get them back before I put the game on every bulletin board in the country."

Her heart dropped to the floor.

"I want one hundred thousand dollars for—"

She gasped. "A hundred thousand dollars!"

"Shut up! You have until Sunday night to get it. That ought to be easy for a rich, hot-shot programmer like you. I'll call back Sunday to tell you where to drop the money. No police! And keep your damn bodyguard in his cage!"

"But—"

The line went dead.

Diana stared at the phone for a moment, then carefully hung up. Her whole body was shaking with the shock of the caller's words. She turned around to face three pairs of curious eyes.

"He claims he has my source codes," she said.

"Repeat the conversation word for word," Angelica commanded.

She did, finishing with, "And then he said no police, and to keep my damn bodyguard in his cage."

"But you don't have a bodyguard," Angelica said.

"Yes, she does," Adam interjected. "Or rather, I

know of one man who's called me her bodyguard on more than one occasion."

Diana snapped her head up and stared at him. "Jim Griegson!"

"Jim? That's crazy," Dan said.

"No, it isn't," Adam replied with a cool smile. "You know about the first run-in Diana and I had with him. We had another one recently, and he wound up looking like a jerk again. Through no fault of mine."

Diana rolled her eyes heavenward.

"He's made it clear he's carrying a grudge against Diana and me. Obviously, this is how he's getting back at us."

"I was wrong when I said it was crazy." Dan spoke slowly, shaking his head. "In fact, he's done it before, although it was just a silly thing at the time. I attended a computer camp last summer, and Jim was there. We all played a game where everyone did programming puzzles and the others had to guess what they'd done. Jim was winning by leaps and bounds, until Stan Fletcher discovered he was swiping the programs during the night to examine them. It was the joke of the camp after that. You know, he never had the creativity to be a first-class programmer, which is probably why he started reporting. His columns are always a little disparaging toward the industry, too. Right, Diana?"

She nodded, realizing how caustic Jim had always been with her. Suddenly she was furious and, at the same time, frustrated by his outrageous demands. "Dammit! I hate the thought of paying him, but what other choice do I have?"

"The hell you'll pay," Adam said harshly.

"But he's going to put it on electronic bulletin boards across the country!" she protested, close to tears again. "Every kid with a computer modem and a phone can just transfer it onto a disk! You don't understand, Adam. The game itself was done, except for the graphics. It's playable. And we can't prove Jim stole the codes, so we can't stop him."

"I've got all the proof I need," he said. "Since I started this, I'll finish it. Somehow. And today." She smiled at his defense of her, until he added, "I believe that will make us even."

"Wait a minute, Adam," Dan said, laying a restraining hand on his brother's arm. "Jim will need a few days just to transfer the codes onto a disk so he can put the game on the bulletin boards."

"Get to the point," Adam said shortly.

Diana was all too aware of his obvious impatience to be gone, and it added to her pain and guilt.

Dan made a face. "His timetable for Diana's payment is probably about the same as the time he needs to get the game ready for the bulletin boards."

"Probably," Diana agreed in disgust. "And another day or so for the worm—"

"You didn't!" Dan said, a huge smile on his face.

Diana grinned, realizing that her one protective measure on the print-out might buy them time for whatever Dan had in mind. She turned to Adam and Angelica. "Before I printed out the program I added a little protection called a worm, a routine that makes the game destroy itself when it's run. When the print-out was stolen, I didn't think about it because all anybody had to do was look at the codes and realize it was a talking adventure game. Then that idea could be stolen. But it will take Jim a while to find my worm, remove it, and get the game running properly."

"And in the meantime," Dan added, "you sell the distribution rights to the game. Then Jim is in a lot more trouble than just breaking and entering, which is probably the worst he can be charged with now. Hold a press conference first thing Monday and publicly announce the sale. Also announce it on all the electronic bulletin boards. Maybe even give a little preview of the game—just enough to make it instantly recognizable. No bulletin-board systems operator will accept the game anonymously then."

"Do you still want the game?" Angelica asked him.

"Of course I still want the game."

She held out her hand. "Give me a dollar. With the understanding that terms and further payment will be negotiated at a later date."

"*Reasonable* terms and *reasonable* payment," Dan said with a grimace, pulling out his wallet.

"Oh, we'll be reasonable," Angelica said sweetly as she took the dollar.

"You'll bleed me dry," Dan grumbled, then said in awe, "A speaking adventure game. I'll be damned!"

Angelica held up the dollar. "We herein witness on this day the transfer of rights to Starlight Software to distribute the game in question. The contracts will be predated just to be safe, and let's all pray we don't have to perjure ourselves in court."

Everyone laughed. Except Adam.

He nodded curtly at his brother and Angelica. "You two get started on whatever you have to do for this. Diana, though, is still vulnerable to a possible personal attack. I'll be staying with her until the press conference. Then my responsibility in this is over."

Twelve

Adam turned out the last of the living-room lights
and settled on Diana's white-and-gray-striped sofa.
He sighed. This certainly wasn't where he'd envisioned spending the first night of his weekend.

Disgusted with his thoughts, he turned his mind
instead to the events of the morning. Each remembered step of Diana's "investigation" of him
only brought more pain. And he welcomed it. He
had been so damn honorable with her. He had
known making love with her meant commitment,
and he had been more than ready for that step.
He had loved her.

He still did.

He knew he should feel nothing toward her now.
Underneath that innocence was a first-class sche-
mer, who had used him. It hurt even to admit
that. He thought of how he'd been toweringly angry at her believing Angelica's accusation. But
while driving back to Oakland, he'd calmed himself enough to think. He had eventually realized

how his brother's machinations could have caused Diana's confusion. So he'd dragged Dan back here to prove his innocence to her. And then he'd discovered the real truth.

All this time she had thought he'd been playing her for a fool, and she had deliberately played him for one. And she'd done it damn well, he acknowledged, because he felt like the world's biggest fool right now.

There was only one disturbing question that continually found its way through his anger. Why had she made love with him the night before? Surely she hadn't meant to go that far. Her inexperience had been obvious and genuine from the beginning. And yet she had given herself so freely and with such joy. With—

Don't be a fool again, he ordered his heart. Of course she didn't love him. That didn't make any sense at all, considering the revelations of the morning. But still . . .

He lay down on his side, trying to get comfortable on his makeshift bed. He thought of the double bed upstairs and its beautiful single occupant, and cursed fervently. He sternly told himself that he only felt this one final responsibility to Diana. He refused to admit he hadn't been able just to walk away this morning. Instead he reassured himself that she needed a protector one last time, and he'd only elected himself to the post since he'd been the one to first provoke Griegson.

In a way, it was the final proof of his innocence and honor, he decided, grimacing. And Diana hadn't protested. In fact, she hadn't said much of anything to anybody, and least of all to him. All afternoon and evening she'd been hidden away with her computers, getting together a preview of the game for Monday's press conference. Angelica and Dan had worked like fanatics to call the press and also settle the details of the agreement between Starlight and Diana. Adam scowled. All he'd done was revise the sketches for the hotel annex and wander around the house checking the locks. Tomorrow and Sunday didn't look to be any different either. Still, Dan's first telephone call had been to the magazine Griegson worked for. Word of the conference must have reached Griegson by now. Things might perk up anytime, Adam thought, smiling grimly. And he was very much looking forward to it.

Thinking again of the excellent sleeping accommodations upstairs, he groaned.

It was going to be a long weekend.

The next evening Diana sighed, and listlessly pushed at the spaghetti on her plate. Her stomach churned at the idea of actually eating.

"Are you planning to starve yourself?" Adam asked brusquely from across the small kitchen table.

She shook her head and forced herself to take a bite of the dinner he'd made. She managed to swallow, although her stomach protested violently. Adam was right, she thought. She'd barely touched anything yesterday, and today had been worse.

It was his unapproachable attitude that had caused her loss of appetite. He was entitled to punish her with his brooding and his coldness. It was the least that she deserved for the way she had hurt him. But how was she supposed to sit across the table from the man who would walk out of her life in two days, and be expected to eat too? That was asking too much of anybody.

"The spaghetti's delicious," she finally said, smiling tremulously. "So is the sauce. What's the recipe?"

"Two large jars of SauceKing with onions," he replied. The corners of his mouth turned up slightly.

Praying his smile indicated a tiny easing of his anger, she risked a stronger one of her own. "I've used that brand and it never tasted this good."

"It's all in the secret herbs," he said, and took a bite of his own dinner.

"Secret herbs?" Good Lord, she thought in amazement, he was actually talking to her. Even teasing her a little.

He nodded. His gaze dropped to her breasts, hidden beneath a cotton shirt, then quickly refocused on her face.

His silence continued, but Diana was satisfied. He had finally spoken to her—even if it was only for a moment—and without being forced by circumstances to do so. And if he'd talked to her once, then he'd talk to her again. Maybe, just maybe, he'd eventually be willing to hear her apology. It was hard to dismiss his looking at her breasts as a sign of renewed interest in her, but she didn't hold out hope for anything more than his accepting her apology. To do so would be foolishness, and she knew it.

To her surprise, her stomach growled a loud request for nourishment. Taking it as a second good sign, she dug into her spaghetti with gusto.

It was almost two o'clock in the morning when

Diana finally gave up on the idea of sleep. With a sigh, she propped the pillows behind her and sat up.

She silently berated herself for disappearing into her workroom after dinner. At the time she had thought it wiser not to press her luck with Adam. Maybe if she had, though, he would have lost control of his tightly held anger. After he had finished yelling at her, they might have been able to reach some level of understanding.

Diana laughed mirthlessly. Not pressing her luck was a very nice excuse for her full-scale retreat this evening. She figured she had a choice. She could continue the little forays of civility like the one at dinner, until the short time she had left with him was gone. Or, if she wanted to come to terms with him within the next twenty-four hours, she could do something drastic.

As she rejected several different ideas, she realized she'd never be satisfied with just an "apology accepted" before his good-bye. She wanted him—in her life and in her bed. She realized, too, that she'd do anything to get and keep him there. Although her experience with men was limited to one, she sensed that the Adam Robertses of this world were few. And more the fool she'd be if she didn't try her damnedest to get him back.

A thought occurred to her, and she grinned. Actually, Adam would be a fool to let *her* get away. After all, she was sweet, innocent, financially independent, and completely in love with him. What more could a man ask for? The true facts were becoming clearer and clearer.

Adam was definitely in need of a rescue.

Diana tossed back the sheet and scrambled out

of bed. As she headed for the bathroom, she decided the simplest and most dramatic way to rescue him from a life without her was to seduce him. She forced away her panic at the thought. Sophisticated women were gutsy, even in situations of great emotional risk. This would be the greatest emotional risk she'd ever endured, but she wouldn't allow that to stop her. One had to risk everything to gain everything.

Twenty minutes later, as she tiptoed out of her bedroom and down the dark hallway, Diana reminded herself to turn on a lamp once she was downstairs. Adam should at least see the seductive Diana, for goodness' sake! She hoped the nightshirt with its bawdy saying was seductive enough. She hadn't owned a nightgown in years. She really had to get a new wardrobe, with lots of feminine lingerie. Adam would probably like that.

She froze, suddenly aware that someone was quietly climbing the stairs. The carpet runner muffled his footsteps, but they still sounded louder than pounding hammers to her frightened ears. Trying to calm herself, she realized that the person on the stairs had to have gone through the living room, where Adam was sleeping. But Adam wouldn't have let Jim get this far, unless . . .

"Adam!" she screamed.

Then she screamed again when the person rushed the rest of the way up the stairs.

"I've got him, Diana!" Adam shouted, slamming her back against the wall. "Call the police!"

"I will . . . if you take . . . your arm . . . from my throat," she managed to gasp out.

The band of iron squeezing off her air supply instantly vanished, and she slumped in relief against the wall. The man was determined to take years off her life one way or another, she thought with irony.

"Are you okay?" he asked, pulling her into a hard embrace. "Did the bastard hurt you?"

"No, the bastard didn't hurt me," she said, winding her arms about his waist. He was only wearing a pair of briefs, and she buried her face against his furred chest. "You only scared me half to death coming up those stairs."

"You scared me half to death screaming like that," he whispered, hugging her even more tightly against him. "We'd better get out of here and call—"

"Adam," she broke in, pushing slightly away from him to look at his face. "I screamed because I thought you were an intruder."

"But you were coming to get me."

"To rescue you." She paused, then decided to take advantage of the opportunity to confess the truth. The whole truth. "For two days I've been walking around here like a little mouse, afraid to make you more angry with me than you already are. But I'm sick of this wall I've put between us, and I can't stand it any longer. I'm sorry I was so suspicious of you in the beginning, and I'm sorry I've acted so stupidly about everything. And most of all I'm sorry I hurt you. But you need rescuing if you think I'm just going to let you walk out of my life on Monday! I love you, dammit, and no amount of righteous anger on your part will change that!"

"I'm not angry with you," he said calmly.

"You're not?" she exclaimed. She searched his

eyes, but it was too dark to read the expression in them.

His answer came when his mouth covered hers in a searing kiss. Her blood throbbed through her veins, and she clung to him, not quite believing he really was in her arms.

"I love you, I love you," she chanted as he strung tiny kisses down her neck.

He raised his head. "I know. It took me a while to realize you never would have risked making love with me if you didn't. Everything fell into place then. In spite of the things you thought I was capable of doing, you fell in love with me. It took an incredible amount of trust to act on that love. You opened yourself up for more hurt than your 'investigation' gave me. Of course, I'm not exactly crazy about being thought of as the dregs of the male species."

"Here comes the yelling," she murmured.

"You're going to be spending quite some time making up for that, you know."

"I'll be the best little maker-upper you've ever seen," she promised, planting kisses across his chest. "In fact, I was about to start making it up to you before you so rudely interrupted me. I was coming downstairs to seduce you into forgiving me."

He chuckled. "I was coming upstairs to seduce you into loving me again, but I like your way better."

Pressing herself against him, she ran her hands over his back, then slid her fingers under the waistband of his briefs. "I can seduce you now."

He sucked in his breath as she skimmed her hands over his buttocks. "Be my guest."

She pulled him down to the hall floor and seduced him with gentle caresses. She seduced him with hot kisses and honest need.

She seduced him with love.

"No silk sheets," she apologized sadly once they were settled in her bed.

Adam burst into laughter. "You're never going to let me forget that, are you?"

"Probably not," she admitted. "Do you suppose we'll ever manage to get to a bed *beforehand*?"

He lazily stroked her back. "Probably not. You're too damn sexy."

And she was, he thought. She had been earthy and innocent and incredibly loving in her seduction of him. Without fail, she made him forget such gallantries as nice, soft beds for her comfort. Of course, this time he had been gallant enough to be on the bottom. It was a terrific sacrifice, and one that would be enthusiastically repeated many times in the future if he had his way.

"Adam? Was I really sexy, or did I just *look* sexy?"

"Sweetheart, that hallway was so dark I thought you were Griegson at first. Naturally, you're a tad sexier than he is—ouch!"

"A tad sexier?" she asked, her fingers poised at his waist to take another pinch.

"You're the sexiest creature in the world," he exclaimed in a loud voice. "And I'm the luckiest man in the world, because you have bestowed your bounteous favors on humble me."

"You bet your bippy, Roberts." She straddled him and bent down to kiss him. Laying her head on his chest delicious minutes later, she murmured, "I don't think I was ever so scared in my life than when I thought I'd lost you."

"You didn't. You couldn't. I love you too much," he assured her. "And I'm going to kill my brother for his part in this mess."

"It's not all Dan's fault. If I had only been open with you from the beginning, we could have straightened this out then."

"I gave that a lot of thought all evening, and I came to the conclusion that I would have needed a lot of convincing if I had been in your place."

"I never believed you were involved in the theft, Adam, and I told Angelica that. Just for a brief instant I . . . wondered. Mostly because Angelica's reasoning fit in with what I'd first thought about you."

"It's behind us now," he said, holding her tightly. "Where it belongs. What do you think of children?"

Her head snapped up. "Children?"

"Sure. How many kids do you want after we get married? By the way, I'll do the dishes and take out the trash if you'll cook. I hate to cook."

To his shock and dismay, she began to cry.

"Diana! Lord, I'm sorry. I rushed you again. . . ."

"No, you didn't," she said, sniffling back her tears. "It's just that I didn't expect you to want to marry me."

"Of course I want to marry you. You don't think I'm going to let all this seducing go to waste, do you?"

She chuckled. "I guess I don't have very much experience in love."

He sighed. "Diana, if you had any more experience I'd be a dead man."

"I'll try to be more careful of your aged condition—"

He pulled her mouth down to his to stop her teasing. As her tongue mated with his, he happily decided he'd created a sex maniac from a shrimp-sitting virgin.

What man could ask for more?

"I hope to hell I never again have to cram two weeks' worth of work into a weekend," Dan said in a tired voice as the four of them sat around the kitchen table Sunday evening. The dinner dishes had been cleared away earlier. "Especially with this one," he added, and pointed a thumb at Angelica, who scowled at him.

"Is everything finally settled?" Adam asked in an obvious attempt to divert the conversation.

As the other three talked, Diana felt a growing tension inside her. Her thief had said he would call this evening, and she'd jumped every time the phone rang. She had no idea why she should be so nervous. After all, she knew exactly what she was supposed to say. She hoped Jim had been scared away when his magazine had been informed about the conference, and now wouldn't even call—

The telephone rang.

Diana whipped around and stared at the kitchen wall phone as it rang again.

"Go ahead, sweetheart," Adam said, giving her a kiss on the cheek. "Answer it."

Taking a deep breath, she rose from the chair and walked over to the telephone. She took another deep breath and picked up the receiver on its fourth ring.

"Hello?" she asked, vaguely surprised that her voice sounded normal. Her hands were shaking.

"Got the money?"

She took a third calming breath and replied, "I'm not paying you. I've sold the game to Starlight Software, and you are now in violation of federal law. We will prosecute. Return the source codes and—"

"I swear I'll put it on the bulletin boards!"

Through the muffling she recognized Jim Griegson's voice, and it sounded high-pitched and desperate. Obviously he had heard about the conference set for the next morning. By now he also must have discovered the program wouldn't run.

"Starlight is previewing the game on the boards beginning tomorrow and—"

The phone went dead.

Diana slowly hung up and turned around. Adam was there, his arms going around her in a secure embrace. Her teeth chattered helplessly in reaction, and she sagged against him.

"Ya done good, kid," Angelica said, patting her on the back.

"Beautiful, Diana!" Dan exclaimed. "You sounded like Angelica. Or a hachet man for the Mafia. Take your pick."

"Don't start, Roberts," Angelica said warningly.

"Don't tempt me, Windsor."

Adam leaned down and whispered, "I think my brother has the hots for her."

Diana burst into laughter. His ridiculous conclusion was exactly what she had needed to dispel the last of her fears.

"What's so funny?" Angelica asked in a suspicious voice.

"I told Diana a dirty limerick," Adam said inno-cently. "Now, if you two will take your squabbling elsewhere, Diana and I would like to go to bed."

It wasn't until after Dan and Angelica had left that Diana discovered Adam had meant for her to go to bed—and sleep. He intended to stay up and guard the house, and no attempts at seduction could convince him otherwise.

She really should be more understanding when her knight was making a rescue, she thought as she finally climbed into bed.

Still, he didn't have to be so single-minded about it.

The night, though, was too quiet to suit her.

And it stayed that way.

look at Adam, who was standing next to the door of the conference room in the hotel. With everything else that had been happening, she had forgotten to warn him about Sir Morbid's penchant for losing his teeth throughout the game. She had honestly meant to. She had a feeling he would make her pay for this too. Good thing she thoroughly enjoyed the punishment.

She also kept her gaze away from the man seated in the last row of the small, laughing audience. Jim Griegson's appearance had surprised her. She really hadn't expected him to show up, although Adam, Dan, and Angelica had. She wondered if he had come in an attempt to throw off suspicion. With so many reporters present, his absence probably would have been noted and commented on. She only hoped the rest of Dan and Angelica's plans continued as well as this part had gone.

"Ladies and gentlemen," Dan said with a flourish as the computer began to play the music of "We Make Excitement," "Starlight Software is pleased to show you a preview of the first talking adventure game, *Knights of the Oblong Table.* And right now, one hundred of the best-known electronic bulletin boards in the country are also previewing the game to their customers, in the first stage of our media blitz. 'Knights' is the product of one of the most creative minds in this business, and you all know her, Diana Windsor!"

Feeling like a dressed-up doll on display, Diana stood and nodded as the reporters applauded and cat-whistled. She wished she'd worn her plain blouse and skirt instead of the vivid red dress Angelica had bought for her. Oh, well, she thought, sitting back down. She was doing things up proper. Besides, Adam had tried to tumble her right back into bed when she'd put the dress on this morning. If only they hadn't had this damn conference. . . .

She brought her attention back to her surroundings when Dan continued speaking.

"Starlight is also pleased to announce that Diana will be a partner in the company. We feel that every department of Starlight will benefit from her knowledge and judgment. Also, Starlight will have exclusive rights to her future games."

A loud buzz went around the room at this second surprise announcement. Diana glanced down at the table to hide her amusement at Angelica's low grumble of disgust. Angelica and Dan had complained loudly about the concessions they'd given each other. Fortunately, those same concessions wouldn't make a difference in Diana's life. Angelica would oversee the partnership, and she, Diana, only had to create her games and make an occasional visit to the company's headquarters in Seattle. As Adam's wife, she probably would have been doing that anyway.

"We expect to have the game in the stores within the next six to eight weeks," Dan said. "But you'll all get a chance to play the preview version today, and we'll be happy to answer any questions you might have."

One reporter immediately stood up. "How long does your exclusive agreement run with Diana?"

"I'll take that," Angelica said before Dan could answer. "Starlight has exclusive rights while Diana is a partner in the company. Should she, for whatever reason, sell her stock, then the rights revert back to her."

"Was Diana given the stock as part of the agreement?"

"Diana was *not* given stock, she bought it," Dan replied.

"Is that true, Diana?" asked another reporter.

"Yes, quite true," Diana said, smiling at the woman. She wasn't about to tell the woman that the money wasn't actually coming out of her pocket. The payments would be diverted from the profits of the game. "I feel Starlight has excellent goals, and I want to be a part of its future. I will have primarily a consultant status, and won't be involved in the daily running of the company."

She gave an inward sigh of relief when the reporters turned their attention back to Dan and Angelica. The rest of the conference continued smoothly under their more expert direction. Once everybody started milling around the room, she slowly made her way to Adam, carefully avoiding Jim Griegson, who was talking to several reporters.

"Sir Morbid loses his teeth?" Adam asked through tight lips.

"I'm sorry I forgot to tell you," she murmured, keeping her gaze on the floor. "If anybody asks, I can always say Sir Morbid was based on Dan."

"You're not getting off the hook that easily. I'm going to torture you senseless for this one."

She smiled at him. "I can't wait."

"Neither can I." He glanced over her head, then looked back down at her. "Get ready. Here comes Griegson."

Drawing her courage from Adam's calm demeanor, Diana didn't turn around, but waited for Griegson to join them by the door. The large potted plant beside her would shield them from the others.

"Very nice, Diana," Jim said when he reached her. "Although the game is a little silly, isn't it?" he asked with a smirk.

Tilting her head, Diana smiled again. "Did you think that when you were so ready to put it on the bulletin boards, or is it just because we blocked you?"

He gasped, his eyes wide with disbelief. "What?" Obviously, he hadn't considered the possibility that he had been found out.

"Don't bother with the act, pal," Adam said. "We know it was you."

Jim's gaze flicked nervously back and forth between the two of them. "As I told you last night," Diana said, "you're in violation of federal copyright laws. That's big trouble, Jim, and I doubt if *CompuWorld* would be happy about one of their reporters stealing a programmer's source codes and then trying to ransom them."

Jim straightened and glared at her. "I have no idea what you're talking about," he said stiffly.

"Don't be a fool," she said in a low voice. "You gave yourself away that first night, when you told me to keep my bodyguard in his cage. Only Adam has ever been called that, and only by you."

She watched the panic flare for an instant in his eyes. Adam crossed his arms over his chest, and she knew he had seen it too.

"Anyone could have heard me say that—"

"I also recognized your voice, in spite of the muffling." She drew in a deep breath and lied. "And then there's the fingerprint the police found. . . ."

"That's impossible!" Jim blurted out. "I—"

"—wore gloves," Adam finished for him.

"You'll never prove it in court!"

Diana tapped her chin, as if in thought. It was time to pull their second bluff. She only hoped Jim didn't call it. "I guess you have nothing to worry about, then, do you? Of course, you won't mind that the police are searching your home and office right now. After all, there's nothing to find, right?"

Sweat began to bead on Jim's reddening face, although he still protested, "That doesn't prove I did it!"

"You have two choices, Jim," she said. "You can deny the theft all the way to court. That's one option. Or you can sign a full confession that will not be shown to anybody as long as you're a good boy. That's option number two. Starlight will not prosecute if you take option number two."

"That's blackmail," Jim whispered.

Adam's smile never wavered as he said, "There is a third option that Diana hasn't mentioned. You can step outside with me. But I don't think you want to do that. I'd make a prosecution lawyer look like a pussycat."

Diana's ears burned as Jim called Adam a filthy name. She glanced behind her and said, "I think you're attracting attention, Jim. Adam and I wouldn't mind the others getting wind of this, but you might. I suggest you decide what you're going to do, and quickly."

"I need time," he whined.

Diana almost felt sorry for him. Almost. She could never even remotely justify his stealing her source codes for ransom. "You have no time, Jim.

I want the confession before you leave here. Otherwise I will prosecute, with Starlight's backing."

"You bi—" At Adam's growl of warning, Jim stopped his curse. "I'll write the damn thing, okay?"

Adam pulled several typewritten pages and a pen from his pocket and held them out to Jim. "No, you'll sign this. You can read it over, if you like, but you can't make any changes."

Jim stared at "his" confession for a long moment, then took it and the pen from Adam. His hands were shaking badly as he opened the folded papers and read their contents. When he was finished, he looked up at Diana. She could easily discern the defeat in his eyes.

"I want to write that I'm signing it under duress."

"No," she said. "You just sign your name and the date. Anything else and I won't accept it. Then I'll prosecute. We're letting you walk away from this with your dignity and your livelihood intact. A signed confession that stays in a locked safety-deposit box is a very small price to pay for what you did, and you know it."

In a fury, Jim signed the confession and shoved it into her hands.

"I hate you," he spat out. "I hate every one of you creeps who think you're so damn smart and talented. But I showed you! I got past your stupid alarm system and stole your codes. You remember that!"

"Don't try anything with Diana. Ever!" Adam said, grabbing Jim by the arm. Jim's face contorted in pain. "We'll have you in jail so fast, you won't know what hit you. And consider yourself lucky, pal, that I don't take you apart right here for what you did. Now, get the hell out!"

Yanking Jim around, Adam stepped to the door. He opened it and shoved the man outside. As the door shut behind him, Adam dusted imaginary dirt off his hands.

"If I had seen that performance the first time we met," Diana said, grinning at him, "I would have realized you're a Sonny Crockett type."

"At least that guy has all his teeth."

He didn't get a chance to say anything more. Angelica and Dan were there, both asking questions at once.

"It went fine," Adam assured them, taking the signed confession from Diana and holding it up. "Diana really backed the guy against the wall." He gave his soon-to-be wife a smacking kiss on the mouth. "I'm just glad she's on my side."

"I wonder what Jim will think when he gets home and discovers the police have never been there," she said.

"Oh," Adam said, "I expect he'll be sufficiently scared to keep his mouth shut and his nose clean from now on."

Grinning at his brother, Adam silently congratulated himself on his nice, neutral answer to Diana. She didn't know it, but she hadn't actually lied to Griegson when she'd said his place was being searched. They hadn't had any real evidence that Griegson had stolen the source codes, but that didn't mean there wasn't any to be found. He and Dan had hired private detectives to search Griegson's apartment first thing that morning. Just before the conference, Dan had gotten a call from them that they had found the source codes.

Adam hadn't told Diana earlier, just in case nothing was found. She probably wouldn't have approved anyway. It was better to let her think her virtuoso performance had set Griegson on the straight and narrow. If the man thought the police had found the source codes and were ready to prosecute at any time, then that was just a little added insurance. A knight had to protect his princess in every way possible.

But he was so proud of her poise during the confrontation with Griegson. He knew she'd been nervous, but she hadn't needed rescuing once. He had, though. He'd barely been able to keep from punching the smirk off Griegson's face. It had only been his love for Diana and understanding her need to handle Griegson herself that had held him back.

"Now that that's over with," he said, interrupting Diana's reenactment of Griegson's breakdown, "when will this damn conference be done? I want to start a honeymoon as soon as possible, with or without benefit of marriage."

"Everyone will be here for another couple of hours at least," Dan said, and laughed. "Or until all the free food and booze are gone."

Adam groaned.

"Besides, there's no honeymoon until benefit of marriage," Diana said sternly. "And there won't be any marriage until you finish the work on that hotel annex and I finish the game."

He groaned again. "Damn! I forgot all about the hotel."

"And I thought I was the absentminded one in the family," Diana said, shaking her head. "Go to the office now, before your poor partner thinks you've deserted him. And I don't want to see you until the annex is done!"

"You're a hard woman, Diana Windsor," Adam grumbled.

"I'm rescuing our honeymoon from interruption, Adam Roberts. Now, get moving."

With a feral grin he pulled her into his arms for a long kiss. Finally he raised his head and asked, "Can we still fool around before the honeymoon?"

She smiled and kissed him again. "Of course. I'm impatiently waiting for lesson number twenty-eight."

"I bet you'll pass with flying colors."

"Silk sheets at last," Diana said with a sigh as she ran her hand over the bedclothes.

"And in a rented condo in Hawaii, with a rented Ferrari down in the parking lot," Adam said, stripping off his suit jacket and tossing it onto a chair. "All your *favorite* things."

She laughed and threw herself exuberantly into his arms. Taken by surprise, Adam staggered backward before regaining his balance. His wife of one day didn't seem to notice as she hugged him.

"You sure know how to make a girl happy," she said.

He gazed down at her shining violet eyes. It never failed to amaze him that she was gentle, yet strong as steel underneath; innocent, yet totally sensual; naïve, yet sophisticated and smart. And she was his—completely and totally his.

His body responded instantly when she kissed him. His hands tightened around her slim waist.

"I'm starving," she murmured.

"For me, I hope," he murmured back, smoothing his hands down the curve of her bottom. "It's been days."

"Actually, it's been days since I ate properly. I really am starved for a good meal."

He slumped, and she slipped out of his embrace.

"We're really going to have to do something about the way you kill the mood," he said, his hands on his hips.

She grinned. "My stomach growling would kill the mood, and at a more strategic moment."

"Very true," he conceded. "We'll rescue your appetite first, and then we'll rescue mine."

Later, Diana drank the last of her coffee and sighed in pleasure. They had eaten dinner in the privacy of their hotel condominium, and she decided they'd spend every meal of their honeymoon here. She and Adam had worked hard to have an uninterrupted two-week honeymoon. As far as she was concerned, it wouldn't be interrupted by anything—not by lying on the beach, or sightseeing, or even dinners out.

Both of them needed to renew themselves after days of exhaustion. Between work and moving Adam's things into her home, they had had to plan a wedding, too. It had been a small one, with just family and a few friends, but she couldn't imagine a more beautiful way to start their life together. Along with a diamond ring and the most revealing negligee she'd ever seen, Adam had also given her another Charlie. As touched as she had been by the other gifts, nothing had meant more to her than his taking the time to hunt through the secondhand computer shops to find her a replacement for the computer Jim Griegson had smashed. The new Charlie now had his own hidden cubbyhole, from which he controlled their home's burglar-alarm system. Dan had hooked him up to a remote telephone line, too. Adam called him his backup knight.

"Everything was delicious," she said, patting her mouth with her napkin.

"My turn to be rescued," Adam said solemnly.

As she gazed into his amused eyes, she decided she couldn't love him any more than at that moment. He was so loving and so gentle. And so patient . . .

She walked around the small table, sat down on his lap, and kissed him for a long time.

Pulling down the zipper of her bright yellow sundress, he said breathlessly, "You princesses really pack a wallop."

"Especially after we're fed," she replied, unfastening the top three buttons of his shirt. She slipped her fingers inside. "I promise I'll make it worth the wait."

THE EDITOR'S CORNER

We have some wonderful news for you this month. Beginning with our October 1987 books, LOVESWEPT will be publishing *six* romances a month, not just four! We are very excited about this, and we hope all of you will be just as thrilled. Many of you have asked, requested, even pleaded with us over the years to publish more than four books a month, but we have always said that we wouldn't unless we were certain the quality of the books wouldn't suffer. We are confident now that, with all of the wonderful authors who write such fabulous books for us and all the new authors we are discovering, our future books will be just as much fun and just as heartwarming and beloved as those we've already published. And to let you know what you have to look forward to, I'll give you the titles and authors of the books we will be publishing in October 1987 (on sale in September).

Before I go on to tell you about the delightful LOVESWEPTs in store for you next month, I want to remind you that Nora Roberts's romantic suspense novel, **HOT ICE**, is on sale right now. As I mentioned last month, it's dynamite, filled with intrigue, danger, exotic locations, and—of course!—features a fabulous hero and a fabulous heroine whom I know you will love. He's a professional thief; she's a reckless heiress looking for excitement. When he jumps into her Mercedes at a stoplight and a high-speed chase ensues, both Doug Lord and Whitney MacAllister get more than they bargained for! I'm sure you will love **HOT ICE**, so do get your copy now!

We start off our August LOVESWEPTs with Patt Bucheister,

(continued)

who has given us another tender and warm story in **TOUCH THE STARS,** LOVESWEPT #202. Diana Dragas can't stand reporters because they destroyed her father's career as a diplomat. This causes problems for the handsome and virile Michael Dare, who is captivated by the beautiful Diana—and is, alas, also a reporter. Still, Diana can't resist this gallant charmer and allows Michael to sweep her away. When she discovers he's misled her, she has to make the most important decision of her life. As always, Patt has created two wonderful people whom we can truly care about.

Peggy Webb's newest LOVESWEPT, **SUMMER JAZZ,** #203, is as hot and sultry as the title suggests. Mattie Houston comes home from Paris looking for sweet revenge on Hunter Chadwick, the impossibly handsome man who'd broken her heart years earlier. Both Mattie and Hunter are certain their love has died, but neither has forgotten that summer of sunshine and haunting jazz when they'd fallen shamelessly in love—and it takes only one touch for that love to be resurrected. But all the misunderstandings and pain of the past must be put to rest before they can be free to love again. This is a powerful, moving story that I'm sure you'll remember for a long time.

Joan Elliott Pickart has always been well loved for her humor, and **REFORMING FREDDY,** LOVESWEPT #204, has an opening that is as unique as it is funny. Tricia Todd never imagined that her physical fitness program—walking up the four flights of stairs to her office—could be so dangerous! Halfway up, she's confronted by a young thief, and she shocks herself as much as the teenager by whipping out her nephew's water pistol. She threatens to shoot Freddy, the young criminal, and gets more than her man—she gets two men. Lt. Spence Walker, rugged, handsome, and cynical, is certain that Tricia, a bright-eyed optimist, is all wrong for him. So why can't he keep away from her? And furthermore, what is she doing when she's mysteriously out of her office at odd hours during the day? Actually, Tricia is doing exactly what Spence told her not to do—reforming Freddy. You'll laugh out loud as Tricia tries to deal with both Freddy and

(continued)

Spence, teaching each—in very different ways—that they don't have to be afraid of love.

Next, Susan Richardson's **A SLOW SIMMER**, LOVE-SWEPT #205, pairs two unlikely people—gourmet cook Betsy Carmody and hunk-of-any-month quarterback Jesse Kincaid. Betsy and Jesse had known each other years earlier, when Betsy was married to another player on the San Francisco football team. That marriage was a disaster, and she wants to have nothing to do with the big, mischievous, and handsome Jesse . . . but he doesn't believe in taking no for an answer and just keeps coming back, weakening her resistance with his sexy smiles and heart-stopping kisses. This is a charming love story, and Jesse is a hero you'll cheer for, both on and off the field.

Do I need to remind you that the next three books of the Delaney Dynasty go on sale next month? If you haven't already asked your bookseller to reserve copies for you, be sure to do so now. The trilogy has the overall title **THE DELANEYS OF KILLAROO**, and the individual book titles are:

Adelaide, The Enchantress
by Kay Hooper

Matilda, The Adventuress
by Iris Johansen

Sydney, The Temptress
by Fayrene Preston

Enjoy!

Sincerely,

Carolyn Nichols

Carolyn Nichols
 Editor
LOVESWEPT
Bantam Books, Inc.
666 Fifth Avenue
New York, NY 10103

It's a little like being Loveswept

SHEER MADNESS
SHEER COLOR
SHEER PASSION
SHEER EXCITEMENT
SHEER INTRIGUE
SHEER ROMANCE

All it takes is a little imagination and more Pazazz.®

Coming this July from Clairol...Pazazz Sheer Color Wash
—8 inspiring sheer washes of color that last up to 4 shampoos.

Look for the Free Loveswept *THE DELANEYS OF KILLAROO* book sampler this July in participating stores carrying Pazazz Sheer Color Wash.

NEW!

Handsome Book Covers Specially Designed To Fit Loveswept Books

Our new French Calf Vinyl book covers come in a set of three great colors— royal blue, scarlet red and kachina green.

Each 7" × 9½" book cover has two deep vertical pockets, a handy sewn-in bookmark, and is soil and scratch resistant.

To order your set, use the form below.

BANTAM
SHOP·AT·HOME
C·A·T·A·L·O·G

Special Offer
Buy a Bantam Book
for only 50¢.

Now you can have Bantam's catalog filled with hundreds of titles plus take advantage of our unique and exciting bonus book offer. A special offer which gives you the opportunity to purchase a Bantam book for only 50¢. Here's how!

By ordering any five books at the regular price per order, you can also choose any other single book listed (up to a $4.95 value) for just 50¢. Some restrictions do apply, but for further details why not send for Bantam's catalog of titles today!

Just send us your name and address and we will send you a catalog!